Books by Anne Warren Smith

Blue Denim Blues
Sister in the Shadow

Sister
in the
Shadow

Sister
in the
Shadow

ANNE WARREN SMITH

Atheneum   1986   New York

Library of Congress Cataloging-in-Publication Data
Smith, Anne Warren.   Sister in the shadow.

SUMMARY: To escape her popular younger sister's
shadow, Sharon escapes for a summer to the Oregon
coast where a job as live-in baby-sitter
for a difficult family gives her an appreciation
for her own assets.
[1. Baby sitters—Fiction.   2. Self-acceptance—
Fiction.   3. Sisters—Fiction]   I. Title.
PZ7.S6427Si   1986   [Fic]   85-20058
ISBN 0-689-31185-0

Published simultaneously in Canada by
Collier Macmillan Canada, Inc.
Composition by Maryland Linotype, Baltimore, Maryland
Printed and bound by
Fairfield Graphics, Fairfield, Pennsylvania
Designed by Marjorie Zaum
First Edition

To Amy & Becca

Sister
in the
Shadow

1

IN THE HIGH SCHOOL CHOIR ROOM, THE LAST NOTES OF "Racka Doo" died away and were replaced by whispers and shuffles. Three down, one to go. These auditions, over and over for the same solo, were boring.

"Good work, Penny." I nodded to my sister as she walked back to her place in the alto section. I stood up and someone groaned.

"Wait a minute. That's not fair," I said. "Just because I'm the fourth one . . ."

"Sharon is right," Mr. Jay said, shaking his head at the groaner. "Come up to the piano, Sharon."

"Give 'em the goods," said a voice beside me. Kate, my best friend, wrinkled her freckled nose and grinned at me.

Once at the piano, my stomach did flip-flops as usual, but a couple of deep breaths helped. "Ready," I said, and Mr. Jay played the opening chords.

A hundred times at home, I'd sung this solo. It was bound to pay off. And the two girls before Penny probably were out of the running. Lacey Storm couldn't help singing through her nose, and Trish Donahay had flatted every high note. So, it was between Penny and me.

The rest of the swing choir sang the chicka chicka's of the background, and then I joined in. It was fun, a peach of a song, jazzy and cute. A certain applause-grabber at the spring concert.

"Nice going," Mr. Jay said when I finished. "Nice going, all of you. But I think Penny has it. She showed a bit more vitality and energy, which are critical for this solo. Now, let's run through the Roger Wagner number we worked on last week."

Back at my seat, Kate turned sideways so I could share Roger Wagner with her. "Good going," she whispered. "You're brave."

"My love is like a river," we sang. I glared at the back of Penny's head. What I'd been suspecting was true. My little sister was wiping me out. Two years behind me, a lowly freshman, and, not only had she won the last solo of the year, she'd made it big all over school.

"Stop there!" Mr. Jay interrupted us. "A ree-vah.

Not riverrr. Ree-vah. Hear it? Go on." We went on and so did my thoughts.

It was as if Penny'd spent all her primary and middle school years preparing for Santiam High. It was a cinch that she'd forgotten who'd taught her how to tie her shoes. Or who'd practically risked her life to rescue her from that homicidal goose in the park when she was eight. Or who'd convinced Mom and Dad . . .

"Rocks of discord should be rah . . . ksof . . . deescor . . . d," Mr. Jay said. "Remember the consonants. Next measure." We went on.

Half the people we knew didn't believe we were sisters. We both had dark hair, but look at hers, bouncing with health while mine languished as if I'd never heard of brushes. Then there were our bodies. I was too tall. And where I was skinny and flat, she was . . .

"Richer, fuller, come on!" Mr. Jay implored us, waving his hands, as if to pull the sound out of our throats.

You could almost say that Penny was the darling of the whole school, including the seniors. Unbeliev able, but true. Tennis champ, drama star, freshman class president. Of course, her schedule was really tough. Three required courses, four periods left for choir, drama, P.E., study hall . . . How she'd ever talked Dad into signing that schedule . . .

"It's going to be inspirational!" Mr. Jay promised as we finished. "Thanks, girls. That's all."

Girls' Swing Choir was the last period of the day. "Got play practice," Penny told me at the door. "See you around six."

I shifted my stack of books to my other arm. "Isn't Mom expecting you to cook tonight?"

She struck herself on the forehead, a future Meryl Streep. "I forgot. Anyway, this is important. Not enough people showed up to paint scenery last weekend. Want to help?"

I shook my head. "Got a paper to write for history." I'd tried out for that play and still thought the director had made a mistake in not choosing me for something. I was avoiding him these days.

"See you later then." She waved and disappeared into the masses of people in the hall.

"Going home?" It was Kate.

"Sure." We went to our lockers and then out into the May sunshine.

"What a waste," she said. "Having to be in school when it's nice outside."

"I'm ready for it to be over," I said. "Are there six more weeks?"

She stopped walking to free her red hair from the shoulder strap of her book bag. "Whew! That pulled," she said. "Six weeks may not be long enough. The folks say I have to get a job this summer. I've

6

been haunting the placement office. Didn't even know there was a placement office till last week."

"I'm tired of high school," I said. "Wish I were done with it."

Kate shook her head. "You'd miss our senior year. It's the best one. So they say." She grinned.

I thought back to the two years of high school, B.P., Before Penny. *Those* had been the best for me. I shortened my stride so she wouldn't have to rush to keep up with my long legs. "Did Penny really sing 'Racka Doo' better than me?"

The longer Kate was silent, the sorrier I was that I'd asked. "I think Mr. Jay had a hard time deciding," she said diplomatically. She turned to look at me. "That kind of song is Penny's style," she said. "Bouncy. You do nostalgia and love songs—pretty things. I'll never understand why you didn't join folk choir instead of swing."

"Yuck," I answered. "There's nobody fun in that choir."

"That's not true," she said. "There are guys in there!" We spent the rest of the walk home, assessing the fun potential of the kids in folk choir.

"Some of them are okay," I admitted as we reached her yard. "But nobody really listens to their part of the concerts."

"You're crazy," Kate said good-naturedly. "Want to come in?"

7

"Have to work on my paper."

"Call me?"

"Sure."

When I got home, Mom was in the living room surrounded by shopping bags and draperies and rugs in myriad shades of blue.

"Hi," she said absent-mindedly, tucking a lock of salt-and-pepper hair behind her ear.

"You're home early," I said. Mom worked part time in the Happy Cooker shop, pretending to be earning money, but actually spending most of it on exotic equipment like crepe makers, pizza stones, and whisks.

"Where's Penny?" she asked. "I got the afternoon off to take advantage of the sale at Attleborough's. It ends today; she has to decide this afternoon before six, so I can take back what she doesn't want."

"Gorgeous color." I patted a furry blue throw rug.

"Should suit Penny's room. Remember, I asked you both last week if you wanted any changes within reason and you didn't care. Penny was going to go with me, but this play practice . . ."

"Guess what, Mom. She's painting scenery. Till six."

"What'll we do? She said she'd be here. Did she forget?"

"I'll choose her new bedroom."

"You can't." Mom didn't respond to sarcasm. She began to stuff things back into bags. "I'll just take these to school. She can come out to the parking lot and choose. Too good a sale to lose out on. Some of these are half price!"

I stomped into the kitchen. I could have used some new stuff in my room. Why had I said I didn't care. Because, right then, I probably hadn't cared.

"She's supposed to cook tonight," Mom said, coming out to the kitchen to get her car keys. "Do you think you . . . ?"

"I've got a paper . . ."

"Oh dear. What's easy? Spaghetti? I can help you as soon as I get back from Attleborough's. If you start the sauce now, you can do your paper while it simmers."

I nodded and reached for a box of Ritz crackers as she left. How come this perfectly good mother never said, "Hi, Sharon, how was your day," so I could tell her I'd had a disappointment, so she could tell me she was sorry and that the choir director must be an idiot? I munched on crackers and opened the cupboard that held the tomato paste. And how could I ask her to feel bad for me at the same time she was supposed to feel good for Penny?

The phone rang. "No, Penny's not home," I mumbled around the crackers. Wonderful voice. Sounded like a young Burt Reynolds.

As I hung up, I saw the pile of mail on the

9

counter. Penny Burgess, Penny Burgess, Penny Burgess. "Miss Teenage Oregon Contest," "Sophisticado Cosmetics," "Smithers Summer School for Models." What was that all about? There was even a personal letter from Penny's old friend who'd moved to Pennsylvania.

Why wasn't there any mail for me? I shuffled through the letters one more time, just in case, then flung them down.

Maybe I'm catching something, I thought as I felt a headache start. I ground the cover off the tomato sauce with Mom's fancy Homemaker can opener and slapped the can down on the counter. Red blobs of sauce flew across the formica. Clumsy.

I didn't even want mail. All I really wanted was to sing one little solo this spring and write my history paper and have a few minutes by myself with my own mother. The phone rang again. For Penny, no doubt. I picked up the receiver and then set it back down. That would fix 'em. Then I picked it up again and dialed.

"Kate," I said when she answered. "I'm making spaghetti sauce. I forget when to add the chocolate chips. With the onions? Or sprinkled on top with the Parmesan?"

CHAPTER

2

"YOU ARE STRANGE," WAS KATE'S ANSWER. "I'M SUR-
prised your mother lets you in her kitchen. What's
new?"

I told her about Attleborough's sale, and she was
annoyed with me.

"Next time your mother feels generous, let me
know," she said. "I'll help you place your order."

"Besides that," I said, bending under the sink to
find an onion, "I'm tired of Penny this and Penny
that. I'm losing my identity."

"Could be worse," Kate said. "She doesn't em-
barrass you in public like little kids do. She lends you
gobs of neat clothes."

"They're always too short for me. Or humiliating.
Her bust is bigger."

"She fixes you up with dates."

"They're always too short for me, too. Besides, they're the ones she doesn't want."

"So? They're male! Besides, she's fun, Sharon. People like her. You have to admit that."

I had to admit that. I decided to change the subject. "Are you really going to get a job?"

"Have to," Kate said. "The folks say it's character-building. Besides, we need money. Having two of us in college, plus me coming up in a year, makes for poverty."

Kate was one of four children. Her kid brother, David, was an afterthought, twelve years younger.

"What kind of work can you get?" I asked.

"Something at a fast-food place. One thing about living in a college town, there are plenty of hamburger joints."

"And plenty of students to work in them."

"But then they go home for the summer. And make room for me," Kate said. "Think you might try to get a job?"

I considered it. The money would be nice. As well as the status. It sounded so mature when someone said they had to go to work. "I'll have to check it out with the folks," I answered. "Remember, I worked a lot for Mom last summer. She'd just started at the Happy Cooker, and she hired me to do housework along with helping her do all the picking and freezing."

"You know how to make jam and stuff," Kate said. "Those things ought to be required in school, instead of algebra."

"If you don't get a job, you can take a class from me," I said. "It'd be fun to do it together."

"You know what would really be fun," Kate said. "Working at Yellowstone, or some resort someplace. Waiting on tables and stuff. Going away for the summer."

"Let's do it." I clutched the phone to my ear. The maturest of mature. To go away!

"I think it's too late now to apply. And they take older students. College students."

"No wonder they leave the Santiam hamburger joints. They go to Yellowstone." How disappointing. "I have to work on my paper, Kate, and make spaghetti sauce." I hung up, feeling grumpy again.

As I chopped the onion, I relived the auditions. "Vitality," Mr. Jay had said. If only I'd put a little more energy into it, I'd have gotten it. Penny wouldn't have cared. She had so much right now.

And I? Dullsville. Non-person. I could just see myself at the senior party next year, sitting in a dark corner, overhearing someone say my name.

"Sharon Burgess?" the other would ask. "Don't you mean Penny?"

"No, there's a sister. Wasn't there? Sharon?"

"Never heard of her," the person would say.

13

I turned the onion around and carved on the other side. My eyes smarted with tears.

I shook the onion bits into a frying pan and went for a Kleenex. If I didn't do something, I'd be a memory people weren't even sure they had. I added oil to the onions and began to chop a green pepper.

The phone rang and I brandished the knife at it, and then whomped it with Mom's biggest whisk. After the fifth ring, I stopped whomping and answered it.

"Where were you?" Kate asked. "Do you and Penny know about *As You Like It?*"

"Why?" I tucked the receiver between ear and shoulder and used the whisk to move the sizzling onions around in the pan.

"There's a director here from a Shakespeare theater in London. He wants to direct *As You Like It.*" The rattle of a newspaper sounded through the phone. "Tryouts are right after school's out. The Recreation Board is all excited. Sounds perfect for Penny."

Turning back to the cutting board, I slashed the green pepper into slivers and dumped them into the pan. "Garlic," I said.

"You're not even listening."

"I'll tell her, Kate. Maybe I'll try out too. I'm surprised the Recreation Board hasn't called us!" I reached for the jars of marjoram and oregano as we hung up.

It was hard to believe, but Attleborough's extended their bedroom sale for Penny. They didn't even wonder why she and Mom had waited till the last day to begin shopping. "The nicest woman," Mom kept saying. "She said she saw Penny in *Auntie Mame* last December and just couldn't believe that a high school girl could carry off that part so well. She said it was a pleasure to be selling rugs and bedspreads to someone with so much talent." She looked around the kitchen. "Smells wonderful in here. What'd you use my big whisk for?"

"I've been trying to get that sauce into stiff peaks," I answered. "Now, it's your turn."

"I couldn't decide anything in the parking lot," Penny said, dragging me upstairs before Mom even understood what I'd said. "We have to try everything out in the room."

She and I spent half an hour before dinner, tossing rugs around, draping bedspreads over the beds. One shade of blue was absolutely terrific. I snuck a quick look at my own room as we went back downstairs. What a relief. It was really okay. Penny's would be flashier now, newer looking, but mine looked comfortable.

My spaghetti was a success. The four of us lingered at the table, feeling a little too full. Penny talked the most, but then, she'd had the most exciting day, as usual.

"Got a nice solo in swing choir," she said.

"You sounded great," I said. "I was even going to clap."

"You were good, too," she said. "Poor Mr. Jay. What a decision for him." She sighed her Meryl Streep sigh.

"You both tried out for the same solo?" Mom asked.

Penny grinned. "Why not? We wanted to bombard him with excellence."

I had to grin, too. No wonder people liked Penny.

"Want to hear my new theory?" Dad started telling us about the different kinds of students he had in his anthropology classes at OSU. He'd decided that kids from eastern Oregon placed more value on individuality because they came from low density population areas. Of course, Penny and I had to stick up for the kids from our side of the state. So it went, until at last Dad pushed back his chair, slipped his feet back into his Birkenstocks and commented that it was amazing that the phone hadn't rung once during dinner. That reminded me of *As You Like It*.

"From London? You're kidding!" Penny ran to the bookcase to get the book of Shakespeare's plays. "It's a good one," she said. "Which do I want, Rosalind or Celia?" She flipped through the pages while Mom and Dad and I gathered up the dishes.

"Look at these pictures," she raved. "These famous actresses."

"And actors," I said, looking over her shoulder.

"Call Kate," Penny said. Her face was flushed and pretty. "What paper was she reading? Ask her when the auditions are. And the performances. I've got to know."

"I might try out, too," I said. But when I dialed, Kate's line was busy. "I'll call her later," I told Penny. "Right now, I've got to do that history paper."

In a few minutes I was sitting on the floor in my bedroom, surrounded by nine thick books, all of which sprouted many colored slips of paper, my unique referencing system. I balanced my typewriter on my lap and wrote "Chinese Labor in Railroad Construction" at the top.

It was amazing that I really got into it, but I must have, for the next thing I knew it was dark outside my window. The phone was ringing, and I had the feeling it had been ringing for some time. I sighed and set the typewriter on the floor. My right leg had gone to sleep and died. Where was everybody? Why didn't Penny ever answer the phone? It was always for her, yet she never answered it.

My headache was back, pulsating with visions of yellow-skinned immigrants marching off a boat in San Francisco Bay. I hopped to the phone in the hall outside my room, groaning with pain as feeling returned to my leg.

"Miss Burgess?" a woman's voice asked.

"Yes," I answered.

"I'm sorry to call in the evening, but you people

are difficult to get hold of. This is Barbara Ramsey from the *Santiam Post*. We've planned a short feature on outstanding teens, and I'd like to set up an interview with you."

"Me?" I asked.

"Is this Penny Burgess?" she asked.

My head throbbed. My leg tingled. "You asked for Miss Burgess," I said stiffly. "It might interest you to know that there is more than one Miss Burgess."

"My mistake . . ." she started.

"Penny is my younger sister," I continued. "And I'm sure she's not interested in doing an interview. She thinks," I touched my right foot to the floor and recoiled at the resulting twinge, "she thinks the *Santiam Post* is only fit for starting fires." Those had been her very words after a bad review of the play before *Auntie Mame*. She'd had a minor role herself, but she thought the reviewer had been unfair to the leading lady.

There was silence on the other end of the line. "Well, thank you." The woman's voice was cold. "I have several other young people on my list who will be interested."

I hung up feeling guilty. I should call her right back. Confess. But I couldn't. It would be too embarrassing. Penny would be furious. I tested my weight on my foot. Pain! How much longer before it came back to life?

It was that woman's fault. Asking for Miss Burgess, as if there was only one of us. Sometimes, I wished there were only one of us. Me. How lovely it would be . . .

I would be The Burgess Girl. Sharon, of course. The one with the lovely voice, chosen for every prom court, sought after by Ivy League schools . . .

But why was this house so quiet? Maybe I *was* the only one left. How awful if something had happened to them. I raced downstairs, gripping the banister, my right leg still unpredictable.

"What's the matter? You see a ghost?" Dad yawned and stretched in his recliner in the living room. A pile of exam papers slid off his lap onto the floor.

"Dad!" I was delighted to see him. "How come nobody answered the phone?"

He yawned again and scratched at his beard. "The phone rang? Guess I dozed off. Your mother drove Penny to the library; she needed to do research for a science project. Last minute, of course. Was the phone for Penny?"

"Sure." Should I tell him what I'd done? He'd be really disappointed in me. I couldn't tell him. I went back up to my room and stepped into the middle of the paper scraps, sprouts of information about Chinese laborers. What a weird thing to have said to that woman. What was the matter with me?

It was early, but I changed into pajamas. Then,

wrapping my robe around me, I sat on the edge of my bed. My leg was better, but now my stomach felt awful. Forget it, I argued. The Chinese laborers are waiting. But I couldn't forget it. You just don't shrug off the discovery that you wish your sister didn't exist.

And in many ways I knew that life without Penny would be awful.

We were friends, Penny and I. We knew each other inside out. We had whole conversations without saying a word.

Except that this year, with both of us in high school, things had been different. Suddenly, she seemed so smart, so poised, so grown up. She was leaving me behind!

She's not doing it on purpose, I told myself. I just have to accept it. She's in the limelight, and I'm in the shadow.

I don't want to be in the shadow, one part of me said.

It's not so bad, my other self argued. Is it?

I got up to get my hairbrush. If only I'd remember to brush five hundred times, maybe I'd grow some hair with body, or even waves. Once Kate had said my hair was like black silk fabric, with threads of gold in it. Now that was a friend, someone who could make thin, limp, and dull sound beautiful.

Brushing would never solve my problems. I dropped the brush into my lap and stared at the wall.

If only Penny and I weren't together so much. Now that we were both in high school . . .

I should go away for the summer. Find a relative to visit.

I considered. They were all on the East Coast. Expensive plane tickets. Still, a possibility. But who? Grandma and Grandpa were planning a trip to Nova Scotia. Aunt Betty was recovering from some kind of surgery. And how would I ever explain this sudden interest in relatives?

There was Kate! Better than a relative. And Yellowstone! I'd call her!

I paused in the dark hallway next to the phone.

How could I have said that to that woman? What if the newspaper held a grudge. Penny would never get another good review.

"Kate," I said when she answered. "We've got to go away for the summer. Yellowstone, or someplace. Because . . . well . . . you won't believe the awful thing I just did."

THE NEXT AFTERNOON, AFTER SWING CHOIR, KATE AND I went to the placement office.

"I had no idea this was here," I said as we walked into the cubicle next to the counseling center.

"Thanks," said an irritable voice that came from behind stacks of forms and letters on a desk in the corner.

"This is Mr. Babcock," Kate said, laughing at my embarrassment.

Mr. Babcock stood up, nodded curtly at me, and sat back down. His bald head shone as if he'd polished it. His glasses glittered at us; his little mouth pursed in disapproval. "No one listens," he complained. "Everyday, there's a message on the intercom. No one hears it."

I had to agree. *I'd* certainly never heard it.

"So now you've decided you need a job. Or did you come in for a chat?" His plump hand dwarfed a ballpoint pen as he tapped it on the nearest stack of papers.

"A job," I said. "For both of us."

"But out of town," Kate said. "Do you ever get information from places like Yellowstone Park?"

"More dreamers," he said. "All I get are the dreamers." He leaned forward and his eyes behind the glasses were intent. "The best jobs are right here in Santiam, you know. This is just as nice as being in a national park. You go away, you get into trouble. Meet the wrong types." He tapped his pen for emphasis.

Kate sighed. "You don't even have information?"

"Sure. Sure, I do." He drew himself up. "Got all the information you'll ever need." He waved his plump hand around his little office and got up to open a file drawer. "You're making a big mistake, little ladies. Your folks know you want to go that far from home?"

I glanced at Kate. "Not yet," I answered. "But . . ."

"See what I mean," he said and slammed the drawer closed. "Now, how about a nice job washing dishes at Pincho's Pizza Palace."

"It's an opening?" Kate asked.

"It was an opening yesterday. Gone now. You wouldn't believe the missed opportunities I see."

"If I'd known," Kate said, "I would have gone there yesterday. I thought you were going to tell me if there was something. I was in last week, remember?"

"It's just as well, Kate," I said. "This way, we can both go to Yellowstone. Please show us your out-of-town files, Mr. Babcock."

He grumbled about our parents and the terrors of going out of town, but finally he handed over a couple of file folders. They were good reading, full of exotic-sounding jobs in faraway places. But it was true that we were too late for any of them. Most said to apply before March 1.

"I wish I'd known about these sooner," I said, and Kate nodded in disappointment.

"Of course," Mr. Babcock said, unpleasantly reminding me he was still there. "They all say that. If only this, if only that . . ."

"What's this?" Kate asked, pulling out a letter. She bent over it, reading rapidly. "Some guy in Brinton Harbor wants a live-in sitter for his three year old. Look, Sharon." She thrust the letter at me, and Mr. Babcock bent over my shoulder.

"Forgot all about that letter," he said. "Came in about two weeks ago. Job is probably gone now."

"He's a fourth-grade teacher," I said as I read it. "They want a sitter so the mother will get some rest."

24

I looked at Kate. "Brinton Harbor isn't far away, is it? On the coast? But I don't know the first thing about baby-sitting. And it's for only one person. Do you want it?"

"You're the one who needs to get away," she reminded me.

The letter fluttered between my fingers. I wanted to go, but I wasn't sure I wanted to go alone.

"Sounds perfect to me," Kate insisted. Her freckles wrinkled together on her nose, as she bent again over the letter. "You survived the perils of my brother when he was three. You can always learn how to take care of a kid. It's just playing, making sure he doesn't run into the ocean, washing his little hands before he eats . . ."

"You'll need to contact this man," Mr. Babcock said, startling me. He stared at me through the thick glasses, as if daring me to forget him again. "Include your references. If you know anyone who'll vouch for you. And your grades. I hope they're not too bad. And work experience. Assuming you've worked before, that is."

"I wish we knew if he's already found someone," I said. "Could I phone him?"

"Better if I do," he answered. "He's given his school number. Perhaps he's still there."

A few minutes later, we knew that Mr. Hanover was still looking for a sitter. "Just a minute," Mr.

Babcock said and covered the phone with his plump hand. He pushed a piece of paper toward me. "Your name. I'll tell him to expect your letter."

"Ah," he said as I wrote on the paper. "It's the Burgess girl, Mr. Hanover. Sharon Burgess." His round face grew pink with delight and he beamed at me. "I think you'll be delighted. This is one of Santiam's top students. Active. Well-liked. She must be very well organized indeed to carry the load she has."

My mouth flew open to stop him, but Kate grabbed my arm and turned me firmly around. "Be quiet," she whispered.

"Well," Mr. Babcock enthused, rubbing his hands together after he put down the phone. "Well, well. I think we just made a sale. Well."

I couldn't look at him. I copied Mr. Hanover's address into my French notebook. Then we left.

When at last we were outside, Kate put her arms around me. I bent my head into her shoulder and let the tears come.

"I see why you need to go," she said and gulped back a sympathetic sob. "It's awful. You're a wonderful person, and nobody knows it. It's not fair."

Tears ran down my cheeks and into my collar as I lifted my head. "I'm not so wonderful," I blubbered. "Sabotaging Penny's chances with the press. Getting a job because Mr. Babcock thinks I'm her."

"You've got to do this," Kate said, sniffling. She handed me a Kleenex and got another for herself. "You can tell him all about *you* in the letter. Even tell him Mr. Babcock was talking about your sister on the phone, if you must. Actually, I think you'd be better than Penny!"

"Never! Penny would be a super baby-sitter, if she ever wanted to do it."

"She'd never want to do it."

"True. I'll write him, Kate." We started slowly across the schoolyard. "It's scary to think of going alone. I wonder what the Hanovers are like. Nice, I hope."

"Fourth-grade teachers are wonderful," Kate said, beginning to smile again. "Remember Mr. Wharton in fourth grade? Our favorite teacher. And three year olds are darling. Even David was cute when he was three. And Mrs. Hanover will bless you every time she runs off to her bridge group. You'll see. The Hanovers will be great!"

4

"THE HANOVERS WILL BE GREAT." KATE REPEATED those words at least five hundred times during the next six weeks. The last time she said them was in the Trailways bus station parking lot. She was there with Mom and Dad to see me off for Brinton Harbor.

It was actually happening. I was going off to foreign lands. Well, at least to the coast, fifty miles away; it might as well be foreign.

I couldn't believe Mr. Hanover had hired me. Kate had forced me to write to him as if I were full of confidence, but he should have noticed all the things I'd left out, like work experience. And he must have wondered why I sounded so different from Mr. Babcock's description.

28

Actually, the Hanovers had been on trial too as Mr. Babcock and Dad checked their references. "One of our finest young teachers," the Brinton Harbor principal had told them. "Goes the extra mile for the kids." Another teacher had written, "I met the Hanovers at our faculty picnic. Tim Hanover is a sweet, well-behaved child. Mrs. Hanover is rather shy, but pleasant. I'd say this was a good opportunity for your daughter!"

The Hanovers had passed the test, and so had I. I just hoped they'd not be too disappointed.

The bus driver smiled at me. "Take your guitar on the bus with you," he said. "Safer for it there. Your tote bag too." He whistled as he hefted my suitcases into the belly of the bus.

"Thanks." As I picked up the guitar, a shaft of June sunlight flashed off a window, momentarily blinding me, making a painful slice inside my brain. Like a laser, I thought. Maybe it could slice away evil thoughts like the ones I kept having more and more often about Penny.

Dad held the guitar for me as I climbed the steps of the bus. He looked like a middle-aged hippie, bearded and sandaled. I was going to miss him. Could I have talked to him about Penny? It was too late now.

"If it doesn't feel comfortable there, call us," he said. "We'll come get you." It was the third time he'd said it.

"The Hanovers sound great," Kate said, which made it five hundred and one for her.

Dad handed me the guitar and slipped his arm around Mom's waist. Was that a tear in Mom's eye? Would she miss me?

She blinked and frowned a little. "Get enough sleep, Sharon. And remember to take those vitamins."

I nodded again. More sleep sounded great. The last weeks of homework had been unreal. Plus, every time I closed my eyes lately, I dreamed of myself in a delightful world without Penny. In control. In demand. In. It was so wrong, but I couldn't seem to stop. The familiar chugging started in my stomach. I sent a panic-stricken look at Kate.

"It'll be fine," she said and jerked her head at me. "I'll write you," she added.

I turned to go in.

"Stop the bus," someone yelled, and four bike riders, brandishing tennis rackets wheeled into the Trailways lot. Penny, adorable in a pink velour tennis outfit with a matching ribbon holding her curls back from her face, leaped off her bike and ran toward me.

"You can't go without a hug from me!"

I grimaced. I thought we'd said good-bye at breakfast. I set the guitar in the aisle and went down the steps to her. It was like a play. The "Leave-Taking," they'd call it. The anxious parents, clutching each other, the supportive best friend, the sister adding noise and costume interest. And at the side, the extras, dressed like passing shoppers, ticket agents, other passengers, all crowding closer to the action. Her arrival had turned my going away into an event. And the main character? Me? Shouldn't I be waving, laughing, throwing kisses?

"Guess it's time to go," was the best I managed.

"Find out what the boys are like in Brinton Harbor," Penny whispered. "Get the kid interested in video games so you can meet boys."

The bus driver slammed the hatch shut and stood at the steps waiting for me to go back in.

I moved up a step, but Penny clutched me again.

"My sister's going away," she wailed. She hugged me hard once more and whispered, "Cross your fingers for the auditions tonight."

"You'll be great."

"Wanta be Celia, not great!"

"You'll be Celia then," I said. I hugged her, sent a quick wave to Mom and Dad and fled. I flopped into the nearest empty seat and maneuvered the guitar case to a spot under my feet. There was time for one last look at Kate before the bus turned into downtown Santiam traffic and they were all out of sight.

I bent to dig in my tote bag, ignoring the smile of the woman across the aisle. I couldn't spend this time chatting; I had too much on my mind.

In an hour and a half, I'd be at Brinton Harbor.

Living with the Hanovers whom I'd never met, taking care of three-year-old Tim, and doing some hard thinking about what was happening to me and Penny. "You feel threatened," Kate had said. She'd taken Introductory Psych and felt like an expert. "You think she's taking your place in school and at home."

"So tell me another one," I'd grumbled. "I know what the problem is. I just don't know what to do about it."

"I know." Kate had patted my shoulder. "Getting away is good. Good for getting perspective."

"Maybe what I'm doing is running away," I'd said. We'd looked at each other in dismay at that and never mentioned it again.

The tempo of the bus motor changed. Now, there was nothing to look at but sheep pastures and little logging communities. If I didn't get bus-sick from the twisty road, I'd be able to study.

The book I pulled from my tote bag was *One Thousand Ways to Amuse Your Pre-schooler*. Would a thousand ways be enough?

Next, I reached for my stack of three-by-five cards and flipped through them. Recipes: play dough, finger paints, sand paint, pudding paint, Ivory Flakes paint. Then there were cards about what to do with popsicle sticks: castles, bridges, insect cages. Next came sandbox toys: sieves, slotted spoons, egg cartons. Water toys: squirt bottles, plastic tubing, paint brushes.

Some of the books I'd read, I wanted to forget. The scary ones with whole chapters on Hostility: Kicking, Biting, Spitting. How to Potty Train the No-stress Way. Accidents: Beans up Noses, Popcorn in Lungs, Fingers in Wall Sockets, Detergent in Stomachs. Not one card came from those books. Instead, all those details were lodged in my brain like worrisome pins pricking me each time I relaxed.

What would Tim Hanover be like? From the letter, I knew his mother was a full-time mother who needed a break. Had Tim driven her to distraction? His father was a fourth-grade teacher who'd be gone a lot, ocean-fishing to earn extra money. Was he avoiding spending summertime with his monster child?

I opened my book. *Fun With Throwaways*. I reached for my pencil and a new three-by-five card.

By the time we reached Brinton Harbor, I had writer's cramp and paralysis of the brain from worrying.

Brinton Harbor was shrouded in fog. Seagulls perching on the old concrete bridge that led into town peered blindly into the mist, barely rousing themselves with weak, uncaring flutters as we passed. The Old Salt Bakery sign appeared and disappeared as a cloud swirled around it. A red light shone half-heartedly above the intersection and then went out as it presumably changed to green. Rubbing at my window to clear it made no difference.

I'd come here to feel better? Left sunshine and summer for this?

"You sure have a cute sister," the bus driver said as he helped me off.

"Thanks," I answered and stepped into the mist.

He got out my suitcases and a few minutes later, in a burst of stinking exhaust, the bus turned the corner and disappeared into the gray.

"Sharon Burgess?"

I turned around.

"Hi. I'm Larry Hanover." The man standing before me looked to be around thirty. He was tall, with brown eyes, thinning brown hair, and a soft mustache. His brown sweater hung loose from slightly rounded shoulders. He looked relaxed and nice.

The fog churned eerily around us as we slid the suitcases into the back of his rusty pickup.

"Play the guitar?" he asked. "You look musical. In fact," he said with a smile, "you look great. Tim's going to like you immediately."

"That's good," I said. "I hope so."

"Cold?" he asked then, seeing me shiver. "Not a nice day. We'll be home in a few minutes. It's just up the hill."

I climbed into the cab and tasted salt on my lips. I could hardly tell him that in spite of his confidence, my shivers were from terror. Beside us, a bunch of tourists moved along the sidewalk toward Sandpiper

Handcrafts and the Old Salt Bakery. They hunched into bulky jackets and looked as grumpy as the gulls had.

"Californians," he said with a grin. "They don't know our good weather's in the fall. And we don't tell them. We have the good times to ourselves." He frowned a little and concentrated on starting the temperamental motor of his truck. "This is my old bus. Gets me to the docks and back. Andrea drives the other one. She and Tim are at home; he's just finished his nap."

It all sounded ordinary and reassuring. I moved my hand to where he couldn't see it, and crossed my fingers.

The motor chugged, and caught, and then he turned it off.

I looked at him in surprise.

"This is a good time to talk a little," he said. "First of all, you should call me Larry. We're informal here."

"Okay," I said.

"I thought I'd prepare you a bit. About Andrea. Tim's mother." He looked away from me, out the window at the fog. "I don't want to worry you, but you should know that hiring you was all my idea. Andrea may seem a little . . . distant at first. Don't let that bother you. She just needs to get used to you, and used to sharing Tim."

I stared at him. "She wanted someone else?"

"Oh no," he answered. "There's no one else. It's just that Andrea is a perfectionist when it comes to Tim and the house. I'll help you all I can these first days. We just need patience." He smiled as if to reassure me. "She wants this to work out too."

Why was my right foot twitching? I tucked it under my left foot and shifted a little in the seat. "Is there something I should do? How should I act?"

"Take it slow at first," he said. "Let her show you how she does things." He smiled again. "I think you'll be great. I'm really glad you're here."

"Thanks." I leaned back against the seat and crossed more fingers.

It took all of ten seconds to drive through Brinton Harbor's business section. I wished I could see better, but as we climbed the hill above the bay, our visibility diminished even more.

"Almost there," Larry said, and my stomach did a Fosbury Flop.

We turned right at a Mini Market sign onto a narrow, rutted road and stopped in front of mist-shrouded, weather-beaten houses.

The front door of the closest house burst open and a child tore out of it.

"Hey there, Tim," Larry yelled and bounded out of the truck to be tackled ferociously around his knees.

Suddenly finished with Larry, Tim scrambled

around the truck to my door. Leaping up and down like a jumping jack, his frantic face appeared and disappeared at the window as he tried to see inside. Giving up on jumping, he beat his fists at the door. "Come out! Come out! Wanta see you!"

All at once, exhaustion swept over me. Had I only traveled fifty miles? It felt as if I had covered half a continent with jet lag, culture shock, the whole bit. What insanity had brought me here? This kid was the kind every smart baby-sitter avoided. Kate's brother, David, had been a cherub compared to this dude. Before my thoughts were finished, there was silence. A woman stood in front of the truck. Tim ran to stand beside her.

Mrs. Hanover. Andrea. I opened my door and stepped out.

She stood like a piece of sculpture, hard and unbending. She wore jeans and a man's plaid flannel shirt, but there was none of Larry's softness about her. Her light-colored hair was fastened back from her face; her eyes were green and cold. Beside her, Tim looked very small.

"Hello, Sharon," she said. There was no smile on her face.

I looked about for Larry. He was at the back of the truck, unloading my suitcases. I slammed the door of the truck behind me and trudged toward her and Tim.

IT WAS SUPPOSED TO BE DIFFERENT, THIS MEETING. I'D practiced how it would go in front of my full-length mirror at home; my smile had beamed promises of fun; my voice had resonated with confidence and gentle affection.

I never expected hostility. Or that Tim would take advantage. The second I got down to his level, he pushed me, and over I went, onto my rear in the driveway.

What would Mary Poppins have done? Where was my spoonful of sugar, my magic carpetbag? I crawled to my feet and brushed gravel off my jeans.

"Timothy Hanover," his mother scolded. "That was very naughty. Tell Sharon you're sorry."

Her voice sounded like a recording.

"Sorry," he said instantly.

"Call me Andrea," she said then. It was an order, not an invitation.

"Sure," I answered. "Nice to meet you."

Larry'd missed the whole thing. He came around the truck grinning as if it were Christmas morning. "Here she is," he chortled. "Did you ever expect a baby-sitter with such pretty brown eyes, Tim?"

Tim stared at my eyes, and Andrea almost smiled. Then, picking up the suitcases, we followed Tim into the house by way of the garage, which had been turned into a sort of storeroom. From there, we entered the kitchen, tiny and immaculate, with frilly curtains and nothing on the counter tops. We crossed the tidy living room, its windows full of mist and trees, its walls strangely bare. Then, one slow step at a time, talking about the weather, and the bus trip, we followed Tim up the narrow staircase to the bedrooms.

There were only two bedrooms, one for Andrea and Larry, the other for Tim and me. So much for privacy.

We were crowded in Tim's room, wedged between the two single beds, two dressers and a toy chest. Under the dormer, a bookcase bulged with toy trucks and wooden puzzles. Cowboys galloped over the bedspreads and more of them rounded up cattle in a big paper mural on the wall. A mobile of whales dangled over one bed; another of starfish and shells hung from the ceiling light.

"I bet you'd like to help her get unpacked," Larry said, "wouldn't you, Tim, old man?" He rumpled Tim's blond hair with his hand until Tim jerked away and slapped his hair back down.

"Let's go, Andrea," Larry said. "Let them get to know each other."

"I hope you'll have room enough for your clothes," Andrea said politely. "In fact," she hesitated a moment, "in fact, since we're not sure this will work out, you might unpack only a few things . . ."

"*Good* idea!" I nodded like one of those dolls whose heads are on wire springs.

When they were gone, Tim faced me with his arms crossed over his chest. "You can't touch my stuff."

"Fine," I answered. "I won't. Which bed is mine?"

He answered by climbing onto the bed under the whales. When he reached behind him for a corner of the cowboy spread, wrapped his arms around it and stuck a thumb into his mouth, he looked less like a monster.

"Tell me what you like to do, Tim," I said. "We have all summer for having fun." I hoisted a suitcase onto the other bed and turned to face him, the word *fun* clanging in my head like an empty cowbell of a promise.

"No," he said around the thumb, gazing at the floor.

"Do you like to play with trucks?"

"Nope."

"You sure? Whose trucks are those in the book-case?"

He shrugged.

"Will you show me some of your toys?"

He jammed his thumb further into his mouth.

Guess he'd figured out my fun potential. "I need a sweater." I opened the suitcase.

Instantly, he was at my side. He plucked things out, tossed them on the bed. "What's this dumb thing?" (my nightie) Whadya bring this for?" (a book) "What's in here?" (my bag of make-up and deodorant)

I grabbed the bag from him. "That's mine. Leave it alone."

"Fiddledum," he said with a sly grin. "Made ya mad."

"You're getting to know each other." Larry lurched into the room with the last suitcase.

"Don't like her," Tim said. He grabbed Larry's hand.

Larry laughed nervously. "Give her a chance, Tim."

"She's mean. She pinched me."

"What?" I turned.

His big blue eyes swam with tears. Penny could not have acted it better.

"Why don't we let Sharon unpack by herself,

41

Tim?" Larry picked Tim up and backed out of the room, still smiling, but his eyes were nervous.

It took a while to unpack, as I decided what to put in the drawers and what to leave in the suitcases. It was a temptation to stay in the little bedroom forever, but finally, there was nothing else I could do there. Things would improve. In a few days, they'd wonder how they'd ever done without me. I shoved my suitcases and the guitar under the beds and went downstairs.

Andrea was in the kitchen, frying chicken.

"Smells wonderful in here," I said, feeling homesick for Mom and our own kitchen. I wondered if Andrea had any whisks.

She looked up from measuring flour into a bowl and sighed. I'd made her lose count.

"Sorry," I said.

She dumped the flour back into the canister. "Tim and Larry are in the backyard."

"I should go there?"

She nodded.

As I walked around the house to the back, I buttoned up my sweater. A bit of sunlight wafted through the mist, and to my right, like a sketch in light charcoal, I saw the outlines of the Brinton Harbor bridge as it spanned the bay. To my left, I heard pounding surf. We were close to the ocean then. When the fog cleared, maybe there'd be a view.

The little yard was ringed by shrubs and was roofed by a huge spruce tree whose branches hung almost to the ground. Tim and Larry sat at a picnic table under the tree. Next to them was a dirt pile covered with a fleet of toy trucks, tractors, and earthmovers. Toys, I thought. The monster does play.

"You look warmer now." Larry rattled his newspaper to the table and smiled at me. Tim bent over a piece of paper, spreading dark smears of crayon across it.

"I'm fine, thanks. I brought you something from Santiam, Tim." I handed him a little box.

"Hey. Super!" he said, taking out a little Matchbox Jeep. He pushed it across his picture on the table. "Broom, broom," he said.

"Thanks," Larry said. "That was nice of you. Have a seat."

We were silent a moment, watching Tim draw a green box around the Jeep on his paper.

"I may go out fishing tomorow," Larry said. "If this fog clears. I'm waiting to hear from my skipper. He makes the decisions. I'm just a deckhand, lucky to get on the *Blue Heron* for the summer."

He rumpled Tim's hair, and Tim absent-mindedly smoothed it back down as he reached for a different crayon. He'd set the Jeep to one side, and his paper was crisscrossed with heavy black and green lines. I wondered what he was drawing, but I knew better than to ask. All the books had agreed about that. Restricts creativity, they'd said.

"It's a baby," Tim said, once again spiting my child-care knowledge. "It fell in the ocean. The mommy can't catch him. "Look!" He dropped the crayon and swooped his hands together, crushing the paper between them.

Larry rose, his face pale. "No, Tim. That's not real, you know. You made that up."

"Wanta do another one." Tim bombed the Jeep with the crumpled picture.

"I'll get more paper." Larry went into the house, and Tim and I stared at each other.

Larry was back before either of us spoke.

"Smells good in there," he said as he laid a sheet of paper on the table. "Chicken." He sat back down. "You seem level-headed, Sharon. That's good. Also, your baby-sitting experience will come in handy."

I opened my mouth, but closed it again. I simply couldn't remind him there was no baby-sitting experience.

"We'll expect you to ask lots of questions at first," Larry continued. "And there'll be free time for you while Tim naps and after he's in bed at seven-thirty. There's a boy your age in the house next door. Have to get you two together."

A boy! Penny would be delighted for me.

"Jeremy won't like her," Tim mumbled as he

bent over his picture. "He's great big. He flies kites."

Larry smiled. "His folks own the local kite shop."

I shivered again. Seemed like a damp day for sitting outside. Maybe they were more used to it than I. Maybe this seemed like a nice day to them.

"Let's show Sharon the path, Tim." Larry jumped up and strode across the yard.

"Wanta go to the ocean," Tim said, running beside Larry and taking his hand. "Wanta play in my fort."

"Maybe tomorrow." Larry smiled down at him. "That was a good one we built. It may still be there; the tides haven't been too high."

"Maybe I can take Tim," I ventured. "It would be fun . . ."

"Not you," Tim said. "You don't know how to play forts."

What could I say? He was probably right.

"I'm hungry." Tim did an about-face and ran toward the house.

"Oh, oh," Larry said, forgetting about showing me the path. "I had orders to keep him out of the kitchen."

I followed them in and watched Larry lure Tim into the bathroom to wash up.

I checked to see if Andrea was measuring anything. She wasn't. "Can I help?" I asked her.

"The lettuce," she said with a sigh. "You could tear the lettuce."

Andrea's kitchen looked as if she'd just cleaned it up. I reached for the head of lettuce.

"You will wash your hands, won't you."

I laughed and turned on the water. She thinks I'm a klutz, I thought. Maybe someday I'd make spaghetti for them.

We ate at one end of the living room at a table that was jammed against a door to the outside. That explained why the entry to the house was through the storeroom.

Larry served our plates, and Tim was quiet for a few minutes. This was a pleasant room, dominated by the bookcase that filled the wall across from me. A driftwood mobile hung in one corner. The rest of the walls were empty. Strange that there were no pictures. Outside the west window, the sun cut through the mist and cast a glow into the room.

"That window needs washing again," Andrea said. "That's the way it is next to the ocean. Salt all over everything."

"Want some salt," Tim said.

"Food first." Larry nodded at Andrea. "Cute."

"Wonder if I turned off that burner." Andrea struggled out of the corner chair and went to the kitchen. "I did," she said as she wedged herself back in. "Don't serve him so much, Larry."

"Here you go, Tim." Larry passed the first plate.

Tim scowled. "Don't like this."

Andrea leaned toward him. "You like chicken. Try a little." She frowned at Larry. "You've given him way too much."

"Catsup." Tim flattened his mashed potato with his hand. "I need catsup."

"Not tonight," Larry said.

Andrea wiped Tim's hands with a paper napkin and squeezed out of the corner chair as Larry handed me my plate.

"Just a little catsup, darling," she said when she returned.

"I do it."

"No. You put too much. I'll do it."

"Be glad when he grows out of this catsup stage." Larry filled Andrea's plate.

"Now, I need a tiny bit of bread." Tim smiled at everyone and licked catsup off his fingers.

"We have something special tonight, Tim."

Tim peeked under the napkin on the bread basket. "Seeds. Yuck!"

"Oh, that's right." Andrea clicked her tongue.

"Aren't little kids the limit?" Larry grinned at me. "Now that you're here, Andrea and I can look forward to going out occasionally." He nodded at Andrea. "Been ages since—"

"I know, Larry. But we can't rush things. We'll have to see how—"

"Don't wanta stay with her," Tim shouted. "She

pinched me." He snuffled and rubbed his eyes as if he were crying.

"He's upset," Andrea said as she came back to the table again. "Don't cry dearest. I brought you some bread."

Larry chewed vigorously and swallowed. "Eat hearty, Sharon. You look as if you could use some extra pounds."

I picked up my fork. My plate looked much too full.

Tim loved the bread. He turned it into a scoop. He dipped it in his milk, then into catsup, then into mashed potatoes. When Andrea gasped, he stuffed the whole thing into his mouth. Catsup, milk, and gravy ran together down his chin.

One wrinkled green pea on my plate held my attention while Andrea got a wet cloth from the kitchen. She ordered Tim to spit everything out, to hold still, to never do that again. When she took the cloth back to the kitchen, I looked up.

He grinned at me.

I grinned back. I'd never let him know how sick I felt.

One thing was becoming clear.

This job was supposed to help me get things into perspective. At that moment, living in Penny's shadow sounded heavenly.

ANDREA PUT TIM TO BED. "JUST WATCH FOR NOW," she said as she was to say, over and over, in the next days.

So I watched as she whisked him through his bath and into pajamas and tucked him in. She was cool efficiency; the bathroom, the bedroom, and Tim were immaculate when she finished.

I watched some more as she made breakfast the next morning, straightened Tim's half of the room, and put out LEGOs for him to play with.

Tim napped after lunch, and I spent the time in the living room with my Gaining Perspectives notebook, not quite daring to curl comfortably into one

49

of Andrea's chairs. The notebook was Kate's idea: for writing about me and Penny. Maybe I'd write a solution—who could tell.

All I wrote that day was an inventory of my clothes closet at home, with "dull," "outgrown," "hate the color," "too young," or "ugly" next to just about everything. I'd use every cent from this job for new clothes.

I doodled a bit and thought about my new life as a working woman. Earning money. Living away from home. I was growing up; it was great. I tapped the pencil against my knuckles, knocking on wood for good luck.

The weather stayed foggy, so Larry stayed in port. He was gone for hours each day though, to clean and repair gear on the fishing boat. "Bill Stannhope is a good skipper," he said one night. "He keeps everything working, including me."

The next days passed the same way. Boring, boring, boring. The only relief was when Larry was home. At the sound of his car, Tim and I would jump up from whatever we were doing to welcome him. We never did that when Andrea came back.

If I'd wanted a course in how to be Betty Crocker or the White Tornado, I'd have been fascinated. Andrea was the mistress of Cleanliness, Tidiness, Efficiency, and Tired Crabbiness. Sure, Tim and I could play, but it had to be neatly, quietly, and out in

50

the yard so the house wouldn't get messed up. We had to stay nearby, so there were no trips to the beach, or anywhere else for that matter. We ate, slept, and played according to a schedule. We changed clothes, washed hands, and put things away. We listened to Andrea sigh if we did anything that changed the plan for the day.

"Today, I'll do those windows. And prune that shore pine. And mend those shirts." Every morning we heard the new list. But there was never enough time for all she'd planned.

What a relief that Larry was there. He talked about how in a few days, now that I was here, Andrea'd be caught up on housework and would find time to relax. It was nice that he kept hoping.

Thursday evening after Tim was in bed, Larry asked me to get my guitar out.

"I used to play a little," he said, cradling the instrument in his arms. "Sold my guitar while I was in college. Do you know any sea chanties?"

I shook my head. "This summer, I'm going to learn some rock strums."

"Sea chanties don't use rock strums." He played a half-dead G chord, then made a face and handed the guitar to me.

"Can you chord while I sing it? It's called "Dark Old Waters." It's not rock, but you might like it. Some drifter down on the docks taught it to me."

The song was about a boatbuilder saying good-bye to the ship he'd just finished building. Half the lines repeated on every verse and, once I figured it out, I sang along with him.

"That's three-four time," he said. "You should be able to do an arpeggio strum to that." He showed me how to move my fingers for that kind of strum, and then we sang the whole thing again.

He cocked his head toward the kitchen where Andrea was still working. "Time to help my better half," he said. "By the way," he added as he got up. "You don't need to learn rock strums; you have a perfect folk music voice."

Funny, Kate had said the same thing. But folk music wasn't where the action was.

Penny's auditions had been Wednesday and Thursday nights, so at ten o'clock Thursday, I called home.

Penny answered the first ring.

"The auditions were terrifying," she babbled. "But they were wonderful! The director is super! He had us reading Shakespeare as if it was easy! Oh, Sharon, I've got to be Celia. I've got to!"

Penny's voice was like a magnet, erasing all the strangeness of the last four days at the Hanovers. "How do you think you did?" I slouched into the chair, all at once not caring about Andrea.

"I read for Celia and for Phoebe." Her voice

52

grew uncertain. "There were so many women there. A lot of competition. There are never enough men trying out, Sharon. Why is that?"

She continued before I could speak. "I met a neat guy. He's a junior at OSU. I told him I'm seventeen and checking out colleges like Willamette and Lewis and Clark. He's darling. Oh, I hope I get that part. I want to be Celia. I'm perfect for Celia."

I couldn't help the wave of envy I felt. How I wished I was perfect for something.

"Mom says remember this is long distance and how is everything there."

I hesitated. How could I say that Andrea wouldn't let me do anything; she was less than ten feet away from me in the kitchen. "It's fine," I said finally. "Yucky weather."

"It's been beautiful here. I've played tennis every morning this week. How's the monster?"

"He's cute, Penny. I like him." It was true, I realized. I also felt sorry for him.

"Met any boys?"

"There's one next door. Haven't met him yet."

"What are you waiting for? If I get this part," she continued without waiting for my answer, "I'm going to really miss you. You always help me memorize my lines."

"You'll find someone—"

"Yes, maybe that guy I told you about. Maybe

we should hang up," Penny said. "Someone might be trying to call."

"Say hello to Mom and Dad. Tell them it's okay here," I said and we hung up.

I got ready for bed, still hearing Penny's voice in my head. Life was so exciting for her. Always new hurdles, new people to meet, new achievements, new applause. My life was never like that.

If things didn't work out with Andrea, I'd be back in Santiam soon. Maybe that wouldn't be so bad.

I folded back the cowboy spread and, in the other bed, Tim turned toward me and snuggled into his pillow. Asleep, he was darling, messed up blond hair, droopy mouth, long dark lashes brushing against his cheeks. Maybe tomorrow I'd get him away from his mother so he'd be able to play like a child for a change. I'd read enough to know that kids needed to cut loose every now and then.

I lay back against the pillow. The wind had dropped. In the distance, the ocean surf rumbled like the sound of cars passing on a freeway. The words to the folk song I'd learned came back to me. "On the dark old waters, all alone. Where you go, go well, and a fair wind home."

The sounds and smells of Brinton Harbor were becoming familiar to me. In a way, I felt at home here. But how I wished Andrea would let me do what I'd been hired to do.

7

MY SLEEP WAS FILLED WITH TURBULENT IMAGES: Penny and Andrea appeared and disappeared and faded into each other so that sometimes I couldn't tell them apart. Tim toppled me over in the driveway again and again. I pulled myself up again and again, still unable to think of anything to say. When I awoke to a sunlight-filled room, Tim stood beside me. It took a moment to realize that he hadn't just pushed me down one more time.

His hand touched my shoulder. "Don't cry," he said softly. "Did you have a bad dream?"

How sweet he looked. I had to forget how awful he'd been to me all night. "Yes, I had a dream."

He frowned and nodded. "Sometimes I have a bad dream. About a little baby who can't find his mommy."

I'd forgotten little kids had nightmares. "I've got to start sleeping better," I said, swinging my feet out of the bed. "You can help, you know."

He frowned at me. "How?"

"By being nice. And playing with me."

"I *have* to play with you," he said. "Daddy went fishing."

"I fixed Larry's breakfast at four. He'll be back tomorrow night," Andrea said, as we met in the kitchen. She looked tired enough to go along with any plan I might have.

"It's a good day for playing outside," I said before I lost my courage. "There's the sand pile, and the toys in it. We can build tunnels and roads." I turned my back to her and dropped bread into the toaster. Would she sense my lack of confidence? Would Tim announce that he didn't want to play with me?

She sipped coffee and was silent. "I have to run a lot of errands this morning," she said finally. "I thought I'd leave Tim here with his dad, that the weather would still be too bad for him to go out fishing. But since he's not here—" She smiled half-heartedly. "Perhaps it's time to give you more to do, Sharon."

She checked on us three times before she left.

Each time, Tim ran to her, whining about something —sand in his eye, or a truck wheel that wouldn't turn, or a hole that filled up with dirt as fast as he dug it.

"Larry and I thought it would be easier than this," she said. "You see what happens. I'll be gone no more than an hour. For heaven's sake, use the hose to wash his hands and feet before he goes into the house. And check the bottoms of your shoes. And be sure he doesn't hurt himself with that shovel."

"Yes, Andrea," I answered over and over, until finally she drove away.

The moment she left, Tim changed. Our dirt pile became a work of art, a masterpiece of tunnels, bridges, and hairpin curves. We had a wonderful time and after a long while, he rocked back on his heels and brushed off his hands. "It's super," he said. "This is fun. I like you, Sharon."

"I'm glad." I grinned at him as I drew another cupful of dirt out of a long narrow tunnel.

"Let's go now." He stood up. "I want to go see my fort."

"Down to the beach?" I got up slowly.

He grinned. "Come on, Sharon." All at once he dashed to the path. "Come on," he yelled once more and disappeared.

I rushed after him. That monkey!

He looked up at me from a curve in the path. "I'm goin' to my fort."

"Wait for me." I zigzagged down the path, running faster and faster, trying to catch up to him. Finally, as we reached the last part, he let me hold his hand.

We burst out of the path onto the open sand of the beach. Bright sunlight made us halt a moment. Then I dropped Tim's hand and ran to the water's edge, scattering a flock of screeching seagulls into the air as I rushed past. The ocean! There was nothing like it! Warm, moist air blew against my left cheek, and I turned my face and breathed it in. In the distance, the surf curled and smashed brilliant white against the sand; here beside us the gentler blue waves of the bay surged forward and back, unveiling sparkles of agates and shells at my feet.

"Where's your fort?" I asked Tim.

But he was gone, running toward a scarecrow of a person who stood dwarfed in the shadow of the highway bridge. I ran after him. He was turning me into a nervous wreck.

"It's Jeremy!" he announced when I finally came huffing up beside them.

"Hi," I said shortly, wanting to scold Tim.

Jeremy's dark eyes studied me from behind thick glasses. I studied him at the same time. He was tall enough to make me feel short! He was made of sharp angles: the knees, the elbows, the glasses, and even the points of hair sticking out at angles from under his purple cap. What a weird cap it was, with a gold wing sprouting over each ear. Amazing that he wore it in public. "Wings of Mercury?" I asked.

He laughed, and I noticed the beginning of a mustache on his upper lip. "Possibly," he said. "Except if they were Mercury's, they'd be on my heels."

I wished he'd stop staring at me. He was definitely not suave. Not Penny's idea of a dream man.

"Where you from?" he finally asked.

"Santiam."

"Really? Knew you weren't from Brinton Harbor. So you're Tim's baby-sitter. For the whole summer?"

"Hope so. If it works out."

"Andrea sure needs some help with this wild animal."

"Sharon's my friend," Tim said. "We came to see my fort. I'm going."

He sped across the sand, and we jogged behind him away from the bridge, toward the ocean. We passed heaps of driftwood half buried in the sand. Huge trunks of trees, some with their whole root systems still attached, lay like the remains of a giant forest across the beach.

Tim ran close to the driftwood, peering at it, shaking his head, and going on. Finally, he found a pile of logs that had been worked into a rough structure, with part of a roof and two complete sides. "My fort," he said, and ducked through an opening.

Jeremy leaped up on top. "I'm the big bad wolf," he called down through a hole in the roof. Jeremy obviously knew how to "play forts."

"Don't let him in," Tim yelled. "He'll eat us up."

Tim dug like a little animal in the floor, occasionally flopping onto his back to grin at the ceiling of his fort. He'd forgotten all about being clean or staying on a schedule. I made scrapers out of boards that were lying around, and Tim and I smoothed one section while Jeremy built the walls thicker. Tim went outside to bulldoze a "garden, for feeding all the soldiers."

After a while, Jeremy came inside the fort and flopped in the sand. "Like your job?" he asked.

"Tim and I had fun today. It's the first time Andrea has left us alone." I tugged at a grassy vine that was growing out of the sand.

"You and Andrea getting along?"

The vine snapped in my hand and I tossed it to one side. "Yes and no. Why?"

"She's weird, that's all." He lowered his voice so Tim wouldn't hear. "Even my mom can't get her to be friendly. And if you knew my mom—" He stretched out as well as he could on the sand floor. Tim bustled outside the fort, making motor noises, pushing sand here and there. "They moved in last September," Jeremy continued when he was comfortable. "Came from near San Francisco. Somebody said she was a famous artist down there."

"I can't believe that. There's not one picture on their walls. Not one!"

He nodded. "I don't believe it either. People like Larry a lot, especially the ones that had fourth graders in his class last year. But she's really weird. It's good they decided to hire you. It'll be nicer for Tim while Larry's out fishing."

I checked Tim's progress in the "garden" through the spaces between the logs. He sure had lots of energy. "I don't know," I said. "Sometimes, she acts as if she's glad I'm here. But mostly, she's not."

Jeremy sat up and banged his head on the roof. He made a face. "Let me outa here. I'm too big for this place." He crawled outside and did calisthenics on the sand.

"Me too," Tim shouted and ran to imitate him.

"Crazies," I muttered as I crawled out of the fort. I wished Jeremy weren't so strange-looking. Penny would have made a reason to meet him sooner, but she would have written him off instantly.

Jeremy looked at his watch soon after that and said he had to go to work at the kite shop. "Maybe you can stop in at the shop sometime," he said. He took off his cap and scratched his head, turning his hair into spikes that reminded me of the Statue of Liberty's head.

"I'm going to be pretty busy with the wild animal," I said with a smile. The perfect light brush-off. Penny couldn't have done it better. "Sorry."

He got the message. "Sure," he said. "See ya later, Tim, old man." A few minutes later, he was out of sight.

All at once, I realized we were off schedule. Andrea would be furious.

"We've got to go back. Hurry, Tim." I tried to take his hand, but he insisted on going his own speed, taking forever to get to the path and then toiling up it as if it were Mount Everest.

His energy had evaporated. I sang songs, recited nursery rhymes, anything I could think of to lure him into a speedier rhythm, but nothing worked. We were halfway up when Andrea met us.

"I was so worried." She ran to Tim.

He burst into tired crying and clung to her. "Want you," he wailed. "Wanta go home."

She carried him up the rest of the hill, scolding me the whole way. "I had no idea where you'd gone. He's exhausted, poor thing. And it's past lunchtime. I was terrified something had happened. This beach is dangerous. You just don't know—"

She didn't finish, but I knew the last word was *anything*.

I was back to just watching when we got to the house. Andrea gave Tim a bath and clean clothes. Gave him his lunch. And a special treat, a Ring Ding, to make up for his awful morning. Then she put him down for his nap. She suggested that perhaps I'd like my time off a little early. She implied that taking time off was what I was best suited for.

I sat in the backyard, too depressed to write in my notebook. I'd messed up my first opportunity to have Tim to myself. At the same time, I'd learned something important. My problem was with Andrea. With Tim, I was okay. That dirt pile under the tree proved it. The imaginary play at the fort proved it. The baby-sitting part of this job was okay for me. I could do it.

But all the ability in the world was no good unless Andrea accepted me. And she'd only do that if she saw that Tim was safe and happy with me.

I began to plan for the afternoon.

AT THREE O'CLOCK, WHEN TIM WOKE UP, I WAS READY. I would ooze cheery confidence. I would clown for him, cajole, coerce. I would be his magic lamp to fun and games and the joy of being a three year old.

"Cockadoodle doo, Tim," I sang as I danced into his room. "I'm your good fairy. It's time to get up and have some *fun!*"

He peered at me through slitted eyes. "You don't look anything like a good fairy."

"Darn." I slapped my forehead. "I forgot my fairy costume. No matter." I snapped my fingers and drew a circle in the air over my head. "Do you see it? My crown? I can do magic. I can make a cookie appear if we go downstairs."

He rubbed his nose and looked slightly interested. Then he slid out of his bed. "I need cookies. Because I been working hard!" He flexed his muscles and pranced out the door and down the stairs.

I picked up his clothes and followed him. So far so good.

Andrea came into the kitchen while I was getting the cookies out.

"Oh," she said. "You got him up. Where are his clothes?"

I held them up for her to see.

"He should be dressed before he has a snack," she said. "And two cookies will be plenty." She filled a pail with water and came back with rags and a bottle of ammonia in her hands. "Going to do those windows in back." She stopped and faced me. "Sharon, if you'd checked with me first, I wouldn't have been so upset this morning."

"I know," I said. "He ran ahead of me. But then we stayed down there to play. I should have brought him straight back."

"What are you going to do now?" she asked, shifting the bottle of ammonia to her other hand.

"I thought I'd give Tim a choice. We can cut up magazines and glue collages, or build something with his LEGOs, or play ball outside. Are those okay with you?"

She nodded. "Put down newspapers if you glue.

In fact, you can do any of those things outside in the backyard. Then I can help if there's a problem and it'll save messing up the house." She waited for my nod, then took her rubber gloves from where they hung under the sink and went outdoors.

"Which sounds like the most fun?" I mopped Tim's fingers with the dishcloth and pulled his shirt over his head.

"Linky Logs," he said. "I want to play Linky Logs."

I guessed we could do that outdoors, too. "Where are they?" I asked.

"Out here." He ran into the storeroom, and I followed holding his pants. "Don't want those. Get away." He twisted away from me and I frowned. If he were naughty, Andrea'd have to dress him after all. Then I remembered my new act and flung the pants in a circle around my head.

"Rid'em cowboy," I said, feeling slightly weird. "Where's the steer these go onto?"

I peered at Tim as if from a long way away. "Ah, there's the beastie."

"Beastie!" His lip curled in scorn. "What's a beastie?"

"You are! Let's see. How do these go on?" I put them over his head and he began to giggle.

"Not like that." He twisted away and grinned at me. He was really cute when he grinned. "They go here." He pointed at his feet.

66

I pretended to need a lot of instructions about putting on pants. By the time he was dressed we were both silly.

"Now, the Linky Logs," he said with a giggle. "Look in that corner, Sharon."

"Are you sure they're here?" I looked at all the things the Hanovers had stored in this room and felt uncertain about pawing through them. There were toys here and there, however, things like a rocking horse that would never have fit into the rest of the little house and a tool set that probably required constant supervision while Tim used it. I peeked over and around things, hoping to find the Lincoln Logs without having to move anything.

"They're here," Tim insisted. "Try that corner."

"Let's take your horse outdoors. He's tired of being in the house."

"No." His face hardened and the cuteness disappeared. "I want those Linky Logs, Sharon."

"I don't think they're here," I said after I'd looked a while. "Let's play something else, Tim."

"Look one more place," he ordered. "Just one more, Sharon." He pointed to the far corner of the storeroom.

"This is the last place. If they're not here, we'll—" I stopped. Stacked in the far corner were canvasses. Paintings, many of them framed. They were beautiful seascapes, with twisted trees, surf pounding against craggy rocks, sand and water glowing red-gold in the rays of the setting sun. Carefully, I set each one out to admire as I worked my way into the corner. In the dim light, I read a signature: A. Madson. "Who did these, Tim?"

"Mommy. You shouldn't touch them."

"How come these are in here? Hidden like this? These are wonderful!"

"Hurry up, Sharon."

"The Lincoln Logs aren't here," I said. "We have to play something else."

He gasped, and I knew Andrea was at the door. She walked in and the door slammed closed behind her.

"What are you doing?" she asked, her voice slicing into the room like a knife. "How dare you go through those things."

I had no defense. I flung my hands helplessly out at my sides and was silent.

"There's been nothing but trouble since you came, Sharon. Tim, go to your room."

Tim sobbed. "I didn't touch them, Mommy. She did it. I didn't. I didn't." He ran into the kitchen, crying.

"I knew they were valuable," I said. "I was very careful." I hesitated a moment while she stared at me. "Oh, Andrea. Tim and I were finally getting to be friends. I'll never be able to take care of him if you make him hate me."

She shrugged as if that were not important. Then

she crossed in front of me and began to restack the paintings as they'd been. Strangely, she turned each one over, as she picked it up, looking only at the backs. I moved to help, but she waved me away. When all was as it had been, she went to the kitchen door. "It's time to have a talk, Sharon."

Each syllable was sharp, wrapped in anger. I followed. Tim was nowhere in sight. I pictured him in his room, hugging the cowboy spread, sucking his thumb.

"Since you arrived, it's been one thing after another," she said, bumping the teakettle against the faucet as she filled it. "It was mostly Larry's idea, hiring you. He has no idea how an extra person adds to the work, instead of diminishing it. I don't want you to stay, Sharon."

The water hissed a little in the kettle, and she turned to the cupboard. "Tea?"

"No thanks." Did one drink tea while being fired?

She pulled the teabag from its envelope with fingers that shook. How could she be so upset? We hadn't done anything wrong that I could see. We'd been having fun, too. Laughing . . .

"You can pack in the morning. The bus leaves for the valley at eleven. I'll drive you to the drugstore."

"Shouldn't we wait for Larry?"

"Larry will agree that I made the right decision. You're a perfectly nice person, Sharon. It's just that I like things done in certain ways . . . We have our routine here, and it's just too hard to fit in another person." She shook her head and smiled a sad smile. "So, in the meantime, till tomorrow morning, it'll be like having time off. Take walks, enjoy being in Brinton Harbor. There's a little museum on Third Street . . ."

Now, she was trying to be nice.

I turned toward the stairs. "Sorry," I mumbled.

"Sharon."

I stopped.

"I'd just as soon you stopped playing with Tim. It excites him."

She walked ahead of me up the stairs. Tim was on his bed, just as I'd pictured him. He pouted at me.

"Sharon couldn't even find the Linky Logs," he said.

Andrea knew where they were in his closet. He went outside to play with them at the table in the yard while she washed windows.

It didn't take long to pack. I'd have to call Mom, tell her I'd be home tomorrow. It was too soon to go home, too soon to go back into Penny's shadow. Frustrating as it had been working for Andrea, at least I'd done it as myself, not as someone's sister. I'd call later, not now.

I walked down the hill into town. The museum was closed. After a long time of aimless wandering, I went into the coffee shop and wrote a letter to Kate on paper napkins.

CHAPTER
9

"DEAR KATE," I WROTE. "ENJOY THIS LETTER, IT'S THE last you'll get. I've been fired.

"I don't know if it was my fault, or if it was inevitable. You see—" I stopped writing to sip at my cup of tea. Yes, I'd made mistakes. Staying down on the beach this morning. Not being assertive enough with Tim this afternoon. If only I'd started out . . .

"Poor Larry. He *was* nice, Kate. So far, our fourth-grade teachers have a perfect record in niceness." I sipped again at the tea. "It's hopeless, Larry," I said silently. "Andrea is a drag." What was her problem, anyway? I tapped my borrowed pencil on the napkins. Jeremy was right. She was weird.

"I met Brinton Harbor's token teenage boy to-

71

day." Then in disgust, I slapped the pencil down on the table. I'd never see Jeremy again. My social whirl in Brinton Harbor had been terminated.

At the Post Office, I bought a stamped envelope and mailed the napkins to Kate. I'd be home before she got them, but it didn't matter.

Five o'clock. I should go back to the lion's den. To the Witch of Weirdness. Was it possible I didn't want to go there? *I am loath to go.* That's what heroines in romance novels said. I was loath to go into the den of lions.

As I trudged along the side of 101, I saw the kite shop. It was an A-frame building, all windows in front. Kites of all shapes and sizes made brilliant splashes of color behind the glass. Windsocks danced from the porch supports, and rainbow streamers flashed from the pointed roof. Was it the thought of seeing Jeremy one more time that drew me? Or was it the lure of the kites? In any case, I went inside.

It was a madhouse of colors in nylon and plastic and silk. Dragons glowered from the ceiling peak; their sixty-foot-long tails swayed and rustled in the draft of the open door. Hand-painted diamond shapes glowed against the dark-stained wood walls. Box kites fluttered beside me and, on the opposite wall, a jet-black octagon with a blazing yellow eye lured me further in.

"Hi, Sharon." Jeremy stood to my left, behind the cash register. His smile looked as if he'd forgotten my Penny-style brush-off.

72

"Oh, Jeremy," I said. "You won't believe what's happened." My words flew out, and he listened as if fascinated, as if it all made sense. Finally, I stopped as I realized there was someone else in the store, a tall, angular woman, standing by the door.

"What a shame," she said. "You've had a bad experience." Her voice was deep and rich, like an opera singer's.

She flipped the sign in the window and turned toward me. "Five-thirty at last. We're closed now."

"I should go." I moved to the door.

"Not you," she said, smiling at me. "You can stay. I'm Jeremy's mother. Mrs. Selivonchick. He told me about you. That you were here."

"Not here for very long," I said and to my horror heard a sob in my voice. I looked away from them both. A moment later, her long arms were around me, and I leaned my head against her shoulder and tried not to cry. I hadn't realized I'd felt so alone.

"Call Andrea, Jeremy," she said. "Ask if Sharon can have supper with us tonight." She pushed me back from her with another smile. "No, I'll call her. You do want to have supper with us?"

I hesitated. I didn't really know them. But my alternative was the Witch of Weirdness. I nodded. "Yes, please."

"Want to look at kites while she calls?" Jeremy looked worried, as if he were afraid I might still burst into tears.

"Sure," I said, hating the quaver in my voice. "Sure," I said again. That was better.

"We've got zillions," he said. "Something for everyone. Some don't fly worth a darn." He pointed to the silky ones. "They're for decoration. But some . . ." His enthusiasm caught me up and made me almost forget about Andrea as he showed me the fighters and the stunt kites, and explained about fabrics and frames and fantastic aerial feats.

"Jeremy's dad is the cook tonight," Mrs. Selivonchick said as she rejoined us. "Soup is his specialty. I hope you like soup."

"Was it okay with Andrea?" I asked.

"Of course," she answered. "Jeremy's going to Oregon State in September. I told her we wanted to know more about living in Santiam."

"You're going to OSU?" I turned to him.

"Yeah," he answered. "Maybe we'll run into each other."

If we did, Penny would die of embarrassment. Maybe if he'd take off that hat . . .

Jeremy drove us up the hill to his house. "Easy to walk," he said. "But usually, we have junk to carry." He waved his hand at the jumble of boxes and kite-related stuff in the car. It felt good to pass by the Hanovers and go into Jeremy's house instead. I wondered what Tim was doing. I wondered if he'd even remember me by next week.

Mr. Selivonchick was tall and skinny, just like

Jeremy and his mother. Being with them made me feel petite, an unusual and nice way to feel. He set down his big soup-stirring spoon and shook my hand. "Company for dinner! Great!" he said.

I'd forgotten what dinner conversations were like without Tim. We talked about the news and politics and kites and tourists and Oregon State and Santiam. We'd finished eating before we got around to discussing the Hanovers.

"Andrea is a strange young woman," Mrs. Selivonchick said. "I heard she was an artist. Well known in the Bay Area. Sold everything she painted." She leaned back in her chair and laughed her deep, rich laugh. "Course, we know the tourists will buy anything."

"There are hundreds of artists on the coast," Mr. Selivonchick said. "Don't think they make much money. She must have been better than the rest."

"I saw some of her paintings." I told them about what had happened in the storeroom before I got fired. "I thought they were beautiful," I said. "I'd never keep them out of sight like that. And she didn't want to look at them. She turned them over as soon as she touched them."

Jeremy's eyes glowed. "I sense a tragedy! Maybe her hands get paralyzed every time she touches a paintbrush."

Mrs. Selivonchick snorted as she got up to put the kettle on the burner. "She just doesn't act like an artist to me. Too rigid. They moved into that house last September. I took some cookies over. Told her to come visit, and bring Tim. She said she was used to being alone." She set four cups out on the counter and turned to us, with her hands on her angular hips.

"This is a small thing, but it was important to me," she said. "She took all the cookies off my plate and put them on one of hers. I said, keep the plate till the cookies are gone. I'd made sure it was a pretty one, you see, and it gives a reason to return the visit. But she couldn't wait to get it and me out of her house."

"Maybe she didn't know your custom, Mom," Jeremy said.

She shrugged and reached for a box of tea. "I got a real unfriendly feeling, I tell you."

I liked the way Jeremy's mother made pronouncements.

Later, we did the dishes, the four of us together, standing around the sink, scraping, washing, drying. It was easy to feel at home.

"So what's your plan, Sharon?" Jeremy asked as he handed me a plate to dry.

"Plan?" I stared at him, wondering if he'd read my mind. I'd actually been wishing I could spend the night with his family.

He handed me another plate. "Larry hasn't fired you yet. He's the one who hired you."

"True, but Andrea said he'd go along with her decision."

Jeremy's dad tossed the sponge into the sink. "It's too bad you can't do something. You're her chance to be happier. But the main thing is Tim. She's always after him about something." He shook his head. "Feel sorry for him."

I nodded sadly. "I like Tim a lot. He can be a sweetheart. He was today." I glanced at the clock on the stove and gasped. "I need to go. She might be waiting up to let me in. It's almost ten."

I thanked them for dinner and gave Jeremy my Santiam phone number. He memorized it and ate the paper. Clown. Would I hear from him in September? Would he even remember me in the excitement of being in college? Penny was the memorable one, not me.

The thunder of the surf filled my ears as I crossed to the Hanover's house. It was dark inside. Andrea must have gone to bed after all. I switched on the light in the storeroom, and there she was, hunched in the middle of the floor. She jerked up to a sitting position. Her face was puffy from crying. One of the paintings was in her arms, the small one of sandpipers.

She shook her head and turned away from me. "You're back. Have a nice time?" Her voice shuddered with tiredness and emotion.

I stepped toward her. She wasn't half as witchy

as I'd made her in my mind. "Did you fall? Are you hurt?"

"Oh, no." She laughed and sobbed in the same breath. "I decided to throw these away hours ago. I started to do it, and then I guess—" She stopped. "I guess—"

"Throw them away!" I peered at her face.

"I couldn't do it," she said in a dull voice. "I don't want to see them anymore. They're just taking up room out here. But I couldn't throw them—" She began to cry again, hunched over the painting, clutching it to her.

"Andrea." I crouched beside her and reached out, then drew back my hand. She was still Andrea, still untouchable. "If you'd let me take care of Tim, you'd have time to draw."

"I can't." The words blurted out, and she sat up straight again and shook her head. "I can't," she repeated with more control. "I've thought of ways to start, but they don't work. That time is over for me, and now I have other things to do. Important things, like taking care of Tim." She looked down at the painting in her lap and traced the line of a sandpiper leg with her finger. "Larry convinced me that hiring you might be the first step. But I couldn't make it work."

She stood up then and laid the painting facedown on the pile. "My life is full enough. Right now,

I can't finish everything that must be done." As she went toward the door, her back and shoulders were straight. She was Andrea again, thinking of her lists, already planning tomorrow's chores.

"I'm going to bed," she announced when we reached the kitchen. Then she swung around to look at me. "Larry thought he was doing the right thing, hiring you. He's a good man; he'll understand what I have to do." Her eyes shone with tears. Then, swallowing back whatever more she wanted to say, she shook her head and went into the bathroom.

CHAPTER

10

"MOMMY MAD AT YOU," WAS TIM'S GREETING AS I
opened my eyes the next morning. "Bad Sharon," he
continued, tugging at his pajama bottoms, which were
twisted around his body. "You didn't even come have
supper with me."

"I ate with Jeremy." I heaved myself out of bed
and stood up. Tired. Sad, because I liked him. If only
I could stay I could make things better for him.

When I told him I was going home, his blue
eyes filled with tears. Real ones. "Stay here, Sharon. I
want you to play with me."

A little late, I thought as I plodded downstairs.
Unless Andrea had changed her mind during the
night.

The shadows under her eyes were darker than

80

ever. She simply nodded when I told her I wanted to walk to the ocean. "I'll be back in plenty of time for the bus," I said as I shrugged into my sweatshirt and windbreaker.

"Want to go," Tim whined. He put his hand into his bowl of cereal and tipped it out on the table. Andrea slapped him, and he was still crying when I went out the door.

The windswept gray ocean reflected the bleakness of my thoughts. The waves were different today, changeable, swamping my feet if I didn't stay alert.

Far away, bobbing like a toy on the ocean, was a fishing boat. Larry's? I'd ask him if they'd fished right off this shore. No, I wouldn't. I'd not see him again. I stomped deep prints into the sand as I strode toward the ocean beach. Andrea was a creep, with her stupid housework and schedules. She said she'd tried; well, it hadn't showed much.

I didn't need Andrea to get jobs. I'd put an ad in the paper as soon as I got home. Larry'd get back, convince Andrea she'd made a mistake, and then they'd find out I was no longer available. That would show them.

I shook off the dream and glanced at my watch. I could get an ad to the newspaper this afternoon. Now that I'd made a plan, I couldn't wait to get started. I turned back toward the bay and the path up the cliff.

At eleven o'clock, the three of us stood silently at

the bus stop in front of the drugstore, pretending to watch the tourists in their never-ending parade. As usual, Tim was like a little puppet around his mother. Would he miss me? I thought he would.

But he'll be all right, I kept telling myself. And I will, too. In a few days, I'd be launched with another family, once again living a life that didn't include Penny. As I climbed the steps of the bus, Tim's lower lip pushed out; his eyes filled with tears.

"Oh, Tim," I said. "I hope you'll still have fun."

"Of course he will." Andrea frowned at me.

"Say good-bye to Larry," I said and went into the bus.

In the valley, the sun was shining. Mom met me at the Santiam bus station.

"Some women can't share their families," she said when I told her about Andrea. "Too bad it didn't work for you, but I'm glad to have you back. I can use your help in the kitchen, the way we did last summer. Would you like to do that?"

"I'm going to look for a baby-sitting job," I said.

Mom looked surprised. "You liked it? Baby-sitting?"

"Very much," I answered. "I'd like to find another full-time job. It'll probably be in town, this time."

Mom sighed. "There goes my good kitchen helper. Do you suppose you could help me until you find something else?"

"Sure," I said.

"I got the part in *As You Like It*," was the first thing Penny said to me. "I'm going to be Celia."

I said, "Oh, fine, Penny. That's what you wanted."

"Aren't you excited?" she asked.

"I have other things on my mind," I answered. "Creating the perfect want ad, for one."

"Baby-sitting." She sniffed. "Bo-o-r-ring."

Kate had started her job at the Taco Temple, but we got together that afternoon. She decided Jeremy was right about some tragedy and spent a long time thinking up reasons for Andrea's need to give up painting. She even thought paralyzed hands were a possibility, but in the form of arthritis. "Are you sure her hands are okay?" she asked. Kate thought Jeremy sounded interesting rather than weird. She was sure he'd call in September; but I kept telling her that we barely knew each other. After all, I'd only spent a couple of hours with him.

"What about you and Penny?" Kate asked then. "Is anything different?"

"How can it be different?" I asked. "I wasn't gone long enough to change anything." I threw Kate's favorite stuffed animal, a purple plush squirrel at her. "I blew it, Kate. I blew my chance to make a difference."

She tossed the squirrel back to me. "It wasn't

your fault, Sharon. Nobody could have worked for Andrea."

I hugged the squirrel to my chest. "I wish I could begin all over again. I wish we could turn back the clock."

Saturday evening passed with me sitting by the phone. There was a chance that Larry might convince Andrea to try again. At ten o'clock, I gave up.

Somehow, Sunday passed while I drew pictures and put them into a note to Tim. It was a fat envelope that I mailed to Brinton Harbor on Monday.

Monday night, Penny talked me into going to the first rehearsal.

"You'll meet some neat people," she said. "Stop mooning around. Besides, your ad won't be out till tomorrow morning's paper, so there's no sense sitting by the phone."

Kate was working, so there was nothing better to do.

The rehearsals were held in the playhouse on campus. As we walked in, a tall graceful man walked toward us.

"Glad to have you with us, Penny," he said. "As I said on the phone, you'll be a wonderful Celia."

"Thanks," Penny said, blushing with pleasure. "This is my sister, Bret. The one I told you about."

His eyes lit up. "Great!" he said, turning to me. "Tell me you'll do it."

"Do what?" I asked.

"Costumes," Penny said. "I told him what you did for my *Auntie Mame* wardrobe."

"You told him what?"

"You're good, Sharon. *As You Like It* needs someone just like you."

"I can't do it." I frowned at her.

"Sure you can. She'll do it, Bret. Don't worry."

"I'm sorry, Bret," I said. "Penny didn't even check with me. I'm getting a job."

He shrugged. "The paycheck beckons more than the play." He went off to greet someone else.

Penny flushed with annoyance. "You know you'll have plenty of time for this, Sharon. Why did you say no? Now I'm in trouble with Bret and this is only the first rehearsal. This is so important to me. Please change your mind."

Penny the Beseecher was hard to resist.

"Please," she repeated. "It would be fun. We hardly ever do things together anymore."

Did Penny miss those close times we'd had? I hesitated. "I know it would be fun," I said.

I'll go to Goodwill with you to find stuff," she said. "And I'll stitch on trims. Whatever."

Penny always promised more time than she had but what the heck. What if my ad had no replys. "All right," I said. "I'll change my mind. Even if I get a job, it can't take all my time."

"Thanks," she said and hugged me. "It'll be fun, and I'll help you, you'll see. You'll be so glad."

Suddenly, she went all sparkly as a young man walked over. "Bret told me you got the part," she said sweetly. "You're the man I fall in love with."

He smiled down at her, entranced, and they walked away without her even telling him who I was.

I looked around for Bret, but I'd have to wait before talking to him. He was ready to begin rehearsal and soon had everyone in the cast seated before him, reading lines of dialogue, analyzing Shakespeare's use of commas, semicolons, and periods as clues to inflection. Very complicated. Very boring.

I looked at my watch. What was Tim doing right now? Getting bathed? Into pajamas? Evenings were a cuddly time when he loved to be held and read to. It was strange that I missed him so much. He'd been such a brat. But not all the time. I shook my head and sat down in the closest chair.

Someone's discarded newspaper was on the chair beside me. I should check the want ads, see if there were any like mine.

"Hi, fair damsel," a deep voice said in my ear. "I'm the melancholy Jaques. From whence comest thou?"

I started and looked up. Bret must have called a break; everyone was walking around, talking in groups.

The young man in front of me was almost as thin as Jeremy. His kind brown eyes gazed near-sightedly at me, begging me to like him, reminding me of puppies in pet shop windows. His long mustache drooped with sadness; he was perfectly melancholy.

"I'm not in the play," I said. "I'll be doing costumes, I guess."

"Very important," he said, and folded his long body into the chair next to mine. "You look friendly. You look intelligent. Anything in the newspaper?"

As I unfolded the paper, a small headline on the front page caught my eye. "Brinton Harbor Craft Subject of Search."

"Oh no," I said as my eyes raced through the article. "High waves and low visibility hamper search efforts by the Coast Guard for the fishing boat, the *Blue Heron*, which was due in yesterday. Two men believed aboard."

The *Blue Heron*. Wasn't that Larry's boat?

"Oh no," I repeated. "It's terrible news." I stood up, and Jaques took the paper from me. "I'm afraid my friend is on this boat."

When he got the paper close enough to his eyes, he was a speed reader. "Call the Coast Guard," he said instantly. "I know where the phone is. Oh, oh," he said, changing his mind. "You can't use this phone; it'll be long distance."

"I'll go home to call." My knees were shaking as

I stood. There must be hundreds of boats, no, it was a small harbor, maybe twenty that went out of Brinton Harbor. The *Blue Heron*. Wasn't that the name Larry had mentioned? It was when we were at the picnic table in his backyard that first day. He'd said the Blue something, but it was probably a common name for a boat.

"Good luck," the wistful young man said. "I hope you find out it's not your friend."

"Thanks," I said. "It's probably not. I'll be back for tomorrow's rehearsal."

By the time I got home, I'd convinced myself the *Blue Heron* was the name of Larry's boat after all. I called the Hanovers first. There was no answer, although I let the ringing go on at least twenty times. Next, the information operator and I worked together to figure out how to spell Selivonchick. After three rings, Jeremy answered.

"It was Larry's boat," he told me. "The Coast Guard has helicopters out searching. Weather's not helping."

"This is Monday. He was due in on Saturday."

"They radioed in on Saturday. They were having good fishing and decided to stay another day. But they should have been in yesterday afternoon."

"What do you think happened?" I caught my breath.

"The waves have been freakish. Big storms out at

sea." He sighed. "If they took a wave in the wheel-house, they lost their power and radios."

"What about Andrea? And Tim? No one answered over there."

"They're at the Coast Guard station. It's up in Paxton Bay."

"Call me, Jeremy, the minute you hear anything. Do you still have my number?"

"Memorized it. Remember? 783-2187. A good number. No indigestion."

I had to smile in spite of my concern about Larry.

Next, I dialed the Taco Temple. Before anyone answered, I hung up. What could Kate do? What could anyone do unless they were in the Coast Guard? I pictured the ocean as I'd last seen it, gray and ominous, and yes, freakish, with the occasional huge wave that had caught me unaware and drenched my feet.

Fifteen minutes later, the phone rang. It was Jeremy.

"Andrea just drove in. They've found the boat and no one's on it. The lifeboat's gone from it, so they must have decided to abandon ship. It's the thing to do, if the power's gone. A dead ship is awful in waves like those. Gets to tossing around . . ."

"So now they're searching for the lifeboat?"

"That's right," Jeremy answered. "Of course, in the dark, and in the rain, the searchlights are almost useless. They'll do better in the morning. Andrea's pretty upset. Mom's gone over to sit with her."

"Oh, Jeremy. What will it be like for Tim . . . without Larry . . . ?"

He was silent. "They'll find him," he said finally.

Half an hour later, I sat before a pile of cookbooks, trying to interest myself in tomorrow's dinner plans. All I could see, however, was a tiny lifeboat tossing on the open ocean.

Penny arrived with Oliver and another guy from the play. The other was Touchstone the clown. Hysterically funny, she said, whether on stage or off.

Touchstone grabbed two apples from Mom's fruit bowl and juggled them before us in the kitchen. "You may have heard," he said, "that we jugglers use three of everything. Not me. Know why?"

"Because you'd drop the third one," I answered. His face fell; I'd stolen his line.

Penny grinned. "We came to get you. It was a drag of a rehearsal, so we're going out for pizza."

"To celebrate the end of the rehearsal," Oliver said. He kept looking at his reflection in the dark glass of the kitchen window.

"And to get a beer," Touchstone added. "How dry I am," he sang as Mom and Dad walked in from visiting the neighbors.

Mom raised her eyebrows. "I suggest you all have your pizza here," she said after the introductions were complete. "It's getting past ten o'clock."

90

"I'm not going anyway," I said. "It's possible that Jeremy may call back." I told them about Larry.

"That's awful," Penny said. "Tragedies happen all the time. But usually not to people you know. Might be good for you to get out, Sharon. Where there's noise and fun."

I shook my head.

"Couldn't the three of us go, Mom?" Penny asked.

Mom shook her head. I could tell she was having second thoughts about Penny being in *As You Like It*. Oliver and Touchstone were too old as far as she was concerned.

"Order a pizza," Dad said, getting the message from Mom. "I'll share the cost. I could go for something with lots of onions and sausage on it."

A few minutes later, the pizza was ordered and the stereo was going full blast. "We have Coke," Mom said firmly to Penny's whispered request that Touchstone have one of Dad's beers. Then she and Dad escaped to the living room and left us in the family room.

"Smile," Penny whispered to me as she and Oliver got up to dance. "You look so sober."

"I can't help it. I keep thinking about Larry."

"You might as well enjoy yourself," she said. "There's nothing you can do. Besides," she bent closer to me, "Touchstone thinks you don't like him."

Touchstone was balancing ten magazines on his

head and trying to do the twist. "He looks devastated," I said.

"Come on, Sharon. I told him you were lots of fun."

"Tonight, I'm not lots of fun, Penny. Sorry."

When the pizza came, I took part of it in to Mom and Dad.

"What do you think, Sharon," Mom said.

"About what?"

"About those guys in there with Penny. The fat one is over twenty-one."

"Penny can handle them just fine, Mom."

"Oh dear," Mom said as I sat down. "Please don't stay in here with us. I'd rather you were in the family room. In fact, Sharon," she paused, "your dad and I are hoping you will be active in this play."

"Oh, Mom." I put the pizza down and mashed at the crust with my thumb. It seemed that everyone but me knew how my life should go. "I guess I'm going to do costumes. I said no, but Penny talked me into it."

"That's great. It'll be fun, won't it?"

"Probably. I just want to be sure to have time to work."

"I don't work you that hard, do I?" Mom grinned at me.

"I mean baby-sitting. My ad comes out tomorrow."

Dad leaned forward. "We'll pay you to work

here, Sharon. That's only fair. So you'll be earning money, and your evenings will be free for *As You Like It*. What do you think? Sound like a good arrangement?"

I shook my head. "I can't believe it. My whole life depends on what's best for Penny."

"That's not true, Sharon." Mom's voice was sharp. "This is simply a family problem that you can help us with. I trust Penny's judgment, ordinarily," she continued, "but this is different from anything she's done before." She and Dad exchanged frowns. I could tell the two of them had made up their minds to worry all summer.

I stood up feeling my eyes burn with unshed tears. "I don't care what I do. I can't even think with Larry out on the ocean somewhere."

"Oh Sharon." Mom's face was contrite. "Of course, you're worried right now. I don't blame you at all."

"The weather's due to clear over there," Dad said. "It'll make all the difference in the world."

"I hope so." I left them and started upstairs. Then I remembered I was supposed to chaperone the family room.

Oliver, Penny, and Touchstone were discussing Bret, the director.

"He has a great sense of timing," Touchstone said, reaching for another piece of pizza. The jerk had stuck a black olive on the end of each finger. "Loved the way he corrected Jaques tonight. Jeez, that guy's a disaster as an actor. He's going to blow the most famous speech in the play."

"Which speech?" Penny asked, smiling at me as if she were glad I was back.

"All the world's a stage—that one. I was in a play with him last fall, and he just can't act."

"I liked him," I said, feeling contrary. "He's nice, and even his mustache is melancholy."

"Penny says you're doing costumes," Oliver said. "I've got some great ideas for mine. Hope you can do all of them in shades of purple. Purple looks great on me. Maybe touches of ermine in the last scene. A dashing hat . . ."

It was the last straw. "I'm going to bed." I tossed my half-eaten piece of pizza back into the box.

"Sharon," Penny wailed. "You're being rude."

"You are all so . . . so petty," I yelled. "Larry might be dead. I'm worried about what will happen to Tim if he is, and I wish I hadn't lost the first job I ever had."

They stared at me as if I'd gone mad. Maybe they were right. "Good night," I said and slammed the door behind me.

94

CHAPTER

11

MORNING FINALLY CAME. AS SOON AS MOM AND DAD left for work, I went to the phone.

"He's still missing," Jeremy told me when I asked about Larry. "They found Bill Stannhope, Sharon. He's . . . he was dead. They don't know what happened. The lifeboat didn't work, or something."

"That makes it definite," I said. "I'm coming back. I don't know what I'm going to tell Andrea, except that Larry wanted me there."

"I'll meet your bus," he said. "I'm glad you're coming."

Penny was more difficult to deal with; all she did was grumble as I talked her into helping me carry the suitcases and the guitar to the bus station.

"Why not call Mom to drive you?" she said.

"Mom's working," I answered. "When a person has a job, they can't be in and out all the time."

The truth was, I didn't want to lie to Mom face to face. It had been bad enough writing the note: "Andrea called. They still haven't found Larry. She wants me to come back."

The bus was on time in Brinton Harbor, and Jeremy stood at the curb, wearing his hat.

"No news," he said in answer to my unspoken question.

"Drive fast, Jeremy," I said as we pushed kite boxes aside and put my things into the car. "Get me there before I change my mind. I still don't know what to say to Andrea. If she throws me out right away, I can maybe catch a bus back to Santiam."

"Andrea's car is gone," Jeremy said as we pulled into the driveway. "She was here this morning."

I climbed out and stared at the empty house. "Now what do I do?"

Jeremy said nothing from his place behind the wheel. He looked as if he was beginning to be sorry I'd come.

"I'll move in," I said.

"What?"

"I'll move in. Be here when she gets back."

"You can't do that. It's house-breaking, or something."

"I don't care." With my options, I shouldn't rule out jail as a warm place to sleep.

96

The door was unlocked, probably the custom in Brinton Harbor since Jeremy didn't seem surprised. He stacked my bags in the storeroom and then went to the door. "You could wait at the shop . . ."

"I'll be fine here."

His eyes were warm behind the glasses. "You're really a nice person, Sharon," he said. "You've only known the Hanovers a week, and it's like you've adopted them as your family."

"I've got to try one more time," I said. "For Larry."

The moment he left, the stillness of the house closed around me. Was it anticipation of Larry's death that I felt? Would he never again come through that door? His wool shirt hung on the hook by the bathroom. I touched it and remembered the last time I saw him wear it. He'd hoisted Tim to his shoulder, and Tim had giggled, waving his arms, trying to touch the top of the door as they ducked through.

I went upstairs. My old dresser drawers were still empty. It was a quick job to fill them and hang the rest of my things in the closet. Tim's bed was still rumpled from his nap. As I smoothed it, the phone rang, making me leap into the air with a scream.

I ran downstairs to the kitchen and watched it ring, not daring to pick it up. How could I explain my presence in this house? All at once I grabbed the receiver. "Hanovers'," I said breathlessly. "This is the baby-sitter speaking."

"This is Reverend Peter Blethel, of the First Methodist Church," a deep voice said. "Have you any news about Larry?"

"No," I answered. "And Andrea's out just now."

"Please tell her that the whole congregation of First Methodist will be praying for Larry's safe return. We have sent the message to our phone outreach committee. By four o'clock, just one hour from now, two hundred and sixty-five members will be praying for Larry."

"That's wonderful," I said. "I'll tell Andrea. Thank you very much."

Before anyone else could call, I called the Coast Guard to see if they had any news of Larry. There was none. I almost asked if Andrea was there, then got scared and hung up.

A car drove up to the house. Again, I panicked. Was it Andrea? I rushed to the kitchen window. No. A heavy woman walked up the driveway and a moment later knocked at the storeroom door.

"Any news?" she asked, wheezing from the exertion. When I shook my head, and explained that Andrea was out, she pressed a pie pan into my hands. "It's chocolate rum," she said. "Sorry about the rum, hope it doesn't offend. It's my best pie, so I got started on it before I thought about the rum."

"Andrea will love it," I assured her, and then hoped I wasn't making Andrea sound like an alcoholic. "I mean, she won't mind . . ."

"My name's on the bottom of the pan," she said. "I sure hope they find him. What a shame. What a shame." She went back to her car, wheezing and shaking her head as she went.

The refrigerator was crammed with food. Fried chicken, two fruit pies, a meatloaf, two identical-looking fruit salads, and enough hamburger casserole for ten people. And now, a chocolate rum pie. I hadn't even had breakfast.

At four o'clock, I was chewing my last bite of apple pie when Andrea and Tim walked in and the phone rang at the same time. I hadn't heard the car. I couldn't believe they were there.

"Hanovers'," I said into the phone, enunciating around the pie, and trying not to look at Andrea's face.

"Sharon's here," Tim hollered and ran to tackle my knees.

"It's for you, Andrea," I said as my legs buckled under Tim's onslaught. I fell onto the floor, whamming my elbow, trying to do it all silently so the person on the phone wouldn't think this was a gymnasium or something. She took the receiver from me and stepped over my legs to drop a bag of groceries and her purse on the counter.

"Hush, Tim," I whispered, hugging him and rubbing my elbow. "Your mommy needs to hear." I kissed his forehead.

"Found! But I just phoned you from the drugstore. They just radioed in? I can't believe it!" She swung around to face us, her eyes bright. "Is he all right?"

Tim and I watched her silently, and I thought it was four o'clock and all the Methodists were praying right then. I hoped they were good at it. Please, God, I thought, adding my prayer to theirs. Let him be all right.

"He's alive," Andrea said. She crumpled to a sitting position across from us on the floor. "I'll meet you at the hospital," she said as Tim crawled out of my lap and went to hers. "I can be there in fifteen minutes. Too soon? Half an hour? I'll be there." She pressed the phone against Tim's back and began to sob.

"They found him," she said finally. "He'd gotten onto one of the buoys near the harbor. Must have spent the night on it. He's very weak. They don't know . . . they're taking him to the hospital." She moved to get up and began to cry again.

"He'll be all right," I whispered.

"Don't cry, Mommy," Tim said, patting the top of her head. "Daddy will be all right."

She got up and hung up the phone. "I didn't expect to see you here, Sharon." She leaned wearily against the cabinet. "Why are you back?"

"It seemed like the thing to do. I thought you might need me."

She blew her nose and wiped her eyes. "I almost

called you last night. I was convinced I was already a widow. And that I should try again to paint. It's the only thing I do well enough to earn money from."

"I'd like to help. If you want me."

She shook her head. "The reason I stopped drawing hasn't gone away. And now, something else is important. When you lose someone, Sharon, you hold on tighter to the ones you have left. I can't share Tim with anyone. I want to hold tight to both of them, to Tim and Larry."

"But Larry wants . . ." I began.

"I want Sharon to stay and play with me," Tim interrupted. "She's fun, Mommy." His eyes filled with tears.

"He's so tired," Andrea said. "Only napped twenty minutes. People kept coming to the door and phoning. We need to go, Tim, and Sharon needs to check out the buses."

"Will I get to see Daddy?" he asked.

She sighed. "I don't know."

"You could leave him with me," I said dully. "You might spend a lot of time just waiting around at the hospital."

She was pushing his arms into his sweater. "I'm sure there's no bus till morning. You'll have to stay here tonight. You can answer the phone while we're gone. I'll call you about Larry's condition as soon as I know. That will be a big help to me, Sharon."

Tim burst into tears. "Ow," he sobbed. "You hurt my finger." He jerked his arm back out of his sweater and waved his fingers in her face.

"Oh, Tim. Not now . . ." Andrea reached for her purse and the keys. "We've got to go."

"Wait, Andrea," I shouted over Tim's howls. "I have to show you something."

I rushed upstairs and came back down with the three-by-five cards. I zipped them through my fingers in my best cardsharp style. "Two inches thick," I said. "Two inches of ways to play with a three year old."

She looked at her watch and took Tim's hand.

I slapped cards onto the table. "Water play. Easy snacks. Best books to read. Finger plays. Take a look." Slap, slap, slap. At least Tim had stopped yelling.

She hesitated, then shrugged. "We have to go in two minutes."

I fanned bunches of cards across the table. She bent over my shoulder, reading. Tim looked at Andrea's face and pulled cards closer to him, pretending to read them too.

"Are they for me?" he asked.

"Yes," I answered. "If I take care of you."

"Read them to me," he demanded. "These are mine, Mommy."

Andrea looked at her watch again, but she was silent.

"There's loads of stuff upstairs," I said. "Paper

102

scraps, straws, old egg cartons. You name it, I've got it. Didn't you wonder why I had so many suitcases?"

Still silence. What was she thinking?

"I know a lot about being safe, too," I said. "What to watch for. What to be careful of."

She pushed the cards together in her hands and straightened them. "You have a lot of information here," she said.

I held my breath.

Tim sat down on the floor with some of the cards. "Mine," he repeated.

She sighed. "I've dragged him everywhere with me today. Jeremy's mother offered to stay . . . I guess I'd decided if it was to be the two of us, he'd better get used to it."

"Let people help, Andrea . . ."

Her eyes filled with tears. "You sound like Larry. He said I take too much on myself." She shook her tears away. "All right. Tim stays here. It's really better. Who knows what we'll find at the hospital. Give Mommy a hug, Tim."

She held him until he squirmed. "Be a good boy."

"He'll be fine," I said.

She turned at the door. "Last night, he was all I had left."

"I know, Andrea. I'll be very careful."

One last look at Tim and, finally, she left.

"Read these to me." He shoved some cards together, bending them, hitting at the ones that fell. He was cranky. Caring for him was going to be no picnic. "Do it now," he demanded.

"The cards are different from a book," I said, listening to be sure Andrea wasn't changing her mind and coming back for him. "We choose one, and it tells us what to do. Are you ready to choose?" He nodded. I shuffled them together and palmed them into fans on the table as I heard the car start up and drive away. "Close your eyes, Tim. Now pick one."

As his hand hovered over the cards, I panicked. What if he chose one Andrea would hate or one we couldn't do today for some reason. I crossed my fingers, but it didn't work. He selected a recipe for no-bake cookies, something that needed special ingredients and a well-rested child.

In the nick of time, I remembered he couldn't read. "Paper chains!" I shouted. "Paper chains! That's perfect!"

His tears vanished. "Paper chains," he repeated and we ran upstairs to get everything we needed.

ANDREA CALLED LATER TO SAY THAT LARRY WAS IN Intensive Care. "He can't talk much, is really weak. He's on IV's. It's unbelievable that he found that buoy and was able to climb onto it."

I gave her a report about the miles of paper chains we were constructing. I left out details of how Tim had pinched his fingers in the stapler three times, cut a little hole in his shirt with the blunt scissors, and had turned his mouth bright red from sucking on a piece of construction paper.

"I'll fix his supper," I said. "And then read a story, and then I'll put him to bed."

"It's good that he stayed home," she admitted. "It would have been hard for him here." She paused.

"Thanks for helping, Sharon. It was nice of you to come back."

Was this Andrea speaking? "No problem," I stammered. "I didn't mind at all."

"Our house is beeyewtiful," Tim said later, admiring paper chains festooned over lamps and table-tops. "Will Mommy like it, Sharon?"

"She'll like it if we pick up all the scraps," I answered. "Let's pick up now and then draw another card."

The next card we drew told us to build a blanket tent, or at least that's what I told him it said. We ate supper on the living room floor under his cowboy spread, which we'd draped over two chairs.

"I like it in here," he said with a contented sigh. "My soft little house. But don't let Mommy scold me," he said, as some chicken fell on the rug.

"I'll clean it up," I said. "Don't worry."

While I did the dishes, he fell asleep under the tent, hugging his teddy bear and a toy truck.

Andrea came home before I'd finished. "What in the world?" she asked, glimpsing the living room.

"Sh," I said. "He's asleep."

"Mommy," Tim said, waking up. He jumped up, and the spread fell down around him, startling him. He burst out crying as he ran to her. "Sharon did it," he wailed. "Don't scold me, Mommy."

"That floor is drafty," she said, picking him up. "Let's put you to bed."

I followed them upstairs and patted the spread back into place on Tim's bed as he got into pajamas. "How's Larry?" I asked.

"Intensive Care for a couple more days, then we'll see. He's got a bad case of pneumonia, but he responded well to the IV's. He's really lucky." She snapped the front of Tim's pajamas.

"Wanta go see Daddy," Tim said.

"Maybe in a couple of days," she answered.

"Can Sharon come see him too?" he asked with a big yawn.

"What is that in your mouth?"

"Paper dye," I answered. "He chewed on a piece of red paper. Did you see all the paper chains we made?"

"Sharon painted my mouth," Tim said. "And she made a big mess."

"And I fixed you a wonderful dinner," I said. "I'll fix you one too, Andrea. There's tons of food."

"I'm hungry," Tim said.

"How can you be?" I asked. "You ate . . ."

"Did not," he pouted. "You don't know how to cook, Sharon."

"Don't you think you should go to bed?" Andrea asked.

"Wanta eat supper," Tim whined.

So I fixed them both dinner. A waste of time because Tim was already full, and Andrea was too tired to taste anything.

Tidying the kitchen later, I thought about the difference between last night and tonight. If I'd stayed home, I'd be at rehearsal, maybe talking to Melancholy Jaques, or getting to know someone else. But today, I'd done things I'd never dreamed I could. I set down the sponge to tick them off on my fingers. I'd lied to Mom, run away from home, broken into the Hanovers' house, done a commercial for myself with three-by-five cards, and charmed a cranky kid into being decent for a few hours.

Not a bad show, Sharon Burgess. Not bad at all!

CHAPTER
13

THE NEXT MORNING, ANDREA ASKED ME IF I'D STAY until Larry came home from the hospital.

"I want to be able to visit him," she said, "and children aren't very welcome. It might be a week."

It was too good to be true! A whole week in which to become indispensable. And this time it would be easier, because Andrea would be away for a lot of it.

After she left, I fanned the three-by-five cards across the table.

They were a toy all by themselves. Tim spent a long time choosing one, sorting them, frowning over them. Finally, he brought one to me.

"It says to take the rocking horse outdoors," I

said. "Poor horsey. How long's it been since he had a romp outside?"

"He likes to stay in the storeroom," Tim said, looking as if the card had made a mistake.

"Let's ask him."

"He bited me," Tim said as we stood by the horse.

"How did he?" I asked. "His mouth doesn't close."

"Here." Tim pointed to the springs holding the horse to the frame.

No wonder Tim didn't like his horse. "Let's try taking him out for a ride," I said. "I'll show you how to keep him from biting you."

After a few minutes, Tim was delighted with his horse. He alternated between stuffing grass in its mouth and catching robbers on horseback while I sat near him in the sun.

I peeked at the back corner of the storeroom when we went back inside. Andrea hadn't destroyed her paintings yet; they were still there.

She came home after lunch, saying that Larry was a little stronger. "We had to tell him about Bill Stannhope," she said. "He can't believe Bill's dead. The lifeboat went in upside down and they both hung onto it anyway. They had their survival suits on, so they could have been okay for a while. The waves were bad though, and Larry lost his grip on the boat and was carried away. Possibly that's what happened to Bill too, and he wasn't lucky enough to find a buoy. It's awful. Bill was going to retire at the end of the season."

She began to repackage the food in the refrigerator after putting Tim down for his nap. "Take some time off," she said, so I carried the guitar out to the path.

There was a log there that was perfect for sitting, with a view of the bay and the bridge. I'd just finished tuning up, when Jeremy called my name.

"Andrea said you'd gone in this direction. Glad you're not in jail." He plopped down on the log beside me and pushed his hat back on his head.

"I'm hired until Larry comes home. Did Andrea tell you about him?"

He nodded. "I sure hope he'll be all right. Was Tim glad to see you yesterday?"

"He was. But Andrea will never know how much fun we have. The minute she walks in the door, he's terrible. He starts fussing, tells lies. Today he even told Andrea I'd been looking through her paintings. She got the funniest look on her face when he mentioned the paintings."

"Maybe they're European art treasures. Stolen from the Louvre."

"And Andrea's a fence!"

We both laughed; it was so preposterous. "What

am I going to do? She thinks I'm an awful baby-sitter. How can I convince her I should stay all summer, the way Larry wanted."

He turned to look at me. "Thought you'd given up on that. Thought you came to rescue Tim from Andrea as a single parent."

"I did. But . . . I'd still like to stay all summer. Andrea's mellowing a little. And besides . . ." I stopped. I couldn't tell him my real reason for staying.

"Think she might decide to take up playing bridge?"

"She might do something, Jeremy. She said she almost called me back herself."

We were silent. Then he grinned at me. "Play something on the guitar."

I looked down at the instrument as if I'd never seen it before. All I knew were dopey love songs.

He touched the strings lightly.

"Do you know how to play?"

He shook his head.

That made it easier. I strummed a chord. "It sounds different out here than in the house. I think the sound of the ocean makes the guitar fuller." I shrugged. "Speaking of the ocean, Larry taught me a sea chanty last week. If you can stand to hear me flub up, I'll try to remember it."

I found the chords and began. "Don't be thinking of me, all away and alone." Jeremy soon joined in, singing the repeating lines. "Dark old waters, all alone. Where you go, go well, and a fair wind home."

"Nice," Jeremy said when we finished. "Guess Larry will take that song personally now."

I winced. "He might not like it anymore."

"Maybe he'll like it more than ever." Jeremy slid down to sit on the ground with the back of his neck against the log. He pulled his hat down over his eyes. He'd soon be asleep. My baby-sitter-style conversation and that ho hum sea chanty had doped him out.

"Strange to think someone wrote a song to a boat," he murmured.

"If you were a boatbuilder, you might."

He opened his eyes. "That's true. It takes ages to build a boat. It'd be hard to send it off to sea, into danger."

"I bet your mom feels that way about you right now," I said. "Sending you off to college."

"Into danger." He grinned and pushed his hat back. "I'm ready to go, too. Can't wait to hit the night life in Santiam."

"The night life? Santiam night life?"

"Got to be better than what goes on in Brinton Harbor. What'd you do while you were home?"

"Went to a play rehearsal."

"See what I mean? Why'd you go to a play rehearsal?"

In a minute, he'd be asking about Penny. No

matter. I'd mention her first to save time. I got up to put the guitar in its case. "My sister Penny's in a play. I went with her."

"You have a sister? Named Penny? You're lucky."

How predictable. I turned. "Why?"

"When you're an only child, sibling rivalry sounds like something fun to do. Is she anything like you?"

When conversation fails, I can always talk about Penny, I thought. I picked up the guitar case. "No, we're different. I've got to get back."

He looked surprised. "Andrea thought you'd be here for an hour."

"I have some stuff to do."

"Meet me tomorrow?"

I turned in surprise. "Meet you?"

"Sure. Ever heard a harmonica virtuoso? I'd like to play that song. We'll put on a show for Larry."

Maybe, after all, there was more for us to do than discuss Penny. "That'll be fun."

After that, Jeremy and I met every day. I sure liked him more than I'd liked Oliver or Touchstone, although I knew what Penny would think. He was too tall, too skinny, too jerky. The hat was ridiculous. The mustache was little more than wishful thinking. The thick glasses were crooked. I could go on and on with the reasons Penny would think he was a waste of time.

The days went by faster than I thought possible.

I'd never been so busy in my whole life, putting tons of energy into doing creative, fun things with Tim, and even doing some of Andrea's housework while she was gone.

"But it's failed," I told Jeremy the day before Larry was to come home. "Tim still cries the minute Andrea walks into the house."

"Doesn't he show her all the stuff you've done? The pictures? The macaroni strings? The clay you baked. The cookies? Those psychedelic string designs? I wish you were my baby-sitter."

"He makes it sound as if I torture him the whole time. I thought of something else, too. Now Larry's not earning the fishing money that was for paying me. It's really hopeless."

I drew in a deep breath of moist salty air. In the waters of the bay below us, two sea lions turned lazily around each other in a watery dance. Gulls screeched overhead, and the bridge stood in sharp relief against the logged-over hills. I'd grown to like being near the ocean. I'd miss so many things.

"It's not helping Andrea that I'm here," I continued. "She's uptight about every bit of dirt or mess. Larry wanted her to relax more; that was the reason he hired me. Maybe someone else could do it. I can't."

Jeremy shook his head. "I wish we knew why she's that way. I think she used to be different."

"Did I tell you I found out how she and Larry

met? He was browsing at an art show down in California where they used to live. He bought three paintings from her. Three! He couldn't even afford them, but anyway, by the time he bought the third one, she said she'd go out to dinner with him. He couldn't afford dinner either. He was in his first year of teaching."

"It was love."

"Yet not one picture is hanging on their walls. Maybe he's the one that changed. Maybe after they were married, he got jealous of her painting. Do you think that's possible?"

"It depends," Jeremy answered. "I'd get jealous if I felt left out. What about you?"

That was one of the good things about Jeremy. We never lacked for things to discuss. We'd never once had to resort to talking about precocious little sisters. Penny would think I was crazy, but I was going to miss him, too.

14

"HEY THERE, BROWN EYES," LARRY SAID TO ME AS HE came into the house. He gave me a big hug.

"I'm glad you're home," I said.

He looked around the little living room and nodded his head. "Feels great!" As he sank down on the couch, I noted the white lines around his nose and the dark smudges under his eyes. He still showed the effects of his ordeal.

Tim came in, dragging Larry's overnight case along the floor. "This weighs more'n a horse, I bet." He abandoned it in the middle of the room and grabbed Larry's arm. "C'mon, Daddy. Come see the big hole Sharon and I digged."

"I need to sit awhile, Tim." Larry circled his

117

arm around him. "Bring me a book, and I'll read it to you."

Tim was back in a moment with a stack of books. "Sharon and me got these at the liberry." He frowned into his daddy's face. "Can you read all right?"

Larry laughed. "Nothing wrong with my eyes. Which one first?"

"It's really time for his nap." Andrea stood in the doorway.

"No, Mommy, no," Tim wailed. He wedged himself tighter against Larry on the couch.

"Let him sleep here with me," Larry said. "We'll nap together today."

Tim ran to get his blanket and Andrea got one for Larry. "I'll start the pot roast," she said. "A couple of hours of good smells from the kitchen should help Larry want to eat. He's still thin."

"I cut up the potatoes and carrots," I said. "Do you need any more help?" I hoped she'd say no because this would probably be my last day to see Jeremy.

"Andrea," Larry called. "Come sit with us for a while. I'll read to you, too."

She laughed. "Read to me, Daddy," she said, mimicking Tim. When I left, the three were cozied together on the couch. They're a family, I thought. They really don't need me.

Jeremy was sitting on the log, waiting for me. "No guitar?"

"I didn't feel like playing today. Just want to stare at the bay—" I stopped. I felt like crying.

"They're sending you home?"

"They haven't said yet. But there's no real reason for me to stay. Even Andrea, with all her weirdness, is still a perfectly good mother for Tim. They're a nice family."

"Darn." Jeremy hunched over his hands and stared at the ground.

"Let's walk down to the beach. It's a nice day. Let's think of all the good things about me leaving." My feet skidded as I started down the path, and I grabbed a tree to stop myself. "Like, it'll be great to have my own room again."

We stepped out on the open sand, and as I looked across at the bridge it blurred into a series of cobwebs, too fragile to hold the traffic that flashed across it. "I don't want to go home," I said, with a sob.

Jeremy took my hand. "It hasn't been a picnic here at the Hanovers. I really wonder why you want to stay."

"I'll tell you." It was time; I'd come close to telling him more than once already. We sat down together on the warm sand, and I smoothed a place in front of me with my palm. "I want to stay here because of my sister." With my finger, I penciled the word *Penny* in the warm sand. "She turns me into a nobody. My whole family does it, but mostly it's her."

He tossed his sneakers to one side and burrowed his feet into the sand. "What happens? You have to wear a name tag so they'll recognize you?"

"It's not quite that bad. Well, almost."

"You never say much about your family. What are they like?"

Where should I start. With Mom? "Mom works at the Happy Cooker selling pots and graters and spices. She likes to cook strange meals and invite people over to eat them. She used to volunteer at the art center. I like her, even though—"

"Even though what?"

"It sounds unfair to say this, Jeremy. But she spends a lot of time thinking about Penny." I was silent a moment. "Then, there's Dad. He's a professor. An anthropologist. He has a beard, and his students really like him. They come for dinner a lot, too. He likes to discuss things—really discuss them, you know what I mean?"

"They don't sound too bad. Go on."

"I've already told you a little about Penny. She's pretty, and fun, and has a ton of friends."

"A ton?"

"She's full of good ideas and fun things to do, and she does everything well, tennis—

"Everything?"

"Yes, Jeremy. And drama, and—

"Does she play the guitar?"

"Well, no. She started once and ran out of practice time. But she sings solos for choir. She's really good."

"Could she take care of Tim?"

I laughed. "He'd drive her crazy. Five minutes with Tim would be five minutes too long for Penny. But that's not her thing, Jeremy. It's not that important."

He pulled his feet out of the sand and brushed them off. "What you've been doing with Tim is important. And hard."

"Penny thinks baby-sitting is Dullsville."

"So that makes it not important?"

"Oh." I turned away, exasperated. "You're just making an argument out this."

He took off his glasses and settled back again in the sand. "Tell me more."

I dribbled sand onto his shirt, and he crossed his eyes at my fingers. "It's simple," I said. "She's practically perfect, and I'm not. It'd be okay if she were ten years older than I am, but she's not. She's only fourteen, and she bowls people over."

"She's fourteen? Thought she was older."

"The phone is always for her. Mom and Dad are always thinking and talking about her. Total strangers rave about her."

"I can't believe a fourteen year old has that much going for her. But say it's true. If you go back, what are you going to do?"

"What?"

He turned on his side, and the sand I'd put on his chest poured inside his shirt. He scratched at his chest and tossed some sand at me. "When you have a problem," he said patiently, "you're supposed to figure out a solution."

"I meant to write in a notebook. I was supposed to gain perspective this summer by writing stuff down. But I haven't had time, and now it's too late."

He sat up and his face was very close to mine. "I've never met your sister, but I bet she's nothing like you."

"That's it, she's not! She's—"

He tapped lightly on my nose with his finger. "I'm not finished. She sounds like she's filled up her life with people and things to do. She sounds like she'd never take time to help a kid like Tim, or to try to understand Andrea. She sounds like she ought to be admiring you!"

My eyes filled with tears, and I busied my hands with brushing sand off my legs. Dear Jeremy. What nice things he was saying. How I wished I could believe him.

AS I WALKED INTO THE HOUSE LATER, TIM WAS SNORING on the couch and Larry and Andrea were sitting at the table with cups of tea. The pot roast smelled good enough to entice Larry to put on ten pounds at one sitting.

"Come join us," Larry said. "Bring a mug."

Here it comes, I thought. At least this time, it won't be as much like being fired. I sat down with them, and Andrea poured my tea.

"I've told Larry what has happened since he left to go fishing," she said.

"It was darned nice of you to come back to help out." Larry put a glob of honey into his tea and stirred it.

"Now we can't decide what to do," Andrea said.

"I know that." I reached for the honey jar. "I only expected to stay till Larry got home."

"Except that I still have the same goal I had when we first hired you," Larry said. "And it's even more important now. I wanted Andrea to have some free time. I still want that, and I hope she'll use it to get her art skills back. Next time something happens to me—"

"Next time?" Tea sloshed from her mug, and she wiped it up with a paper napkin.

"Well, something could happen. I don't want you to have to beg on the street—"

"Is that what you thought I'd do?" She set her mug down with a thump.

He leaned forward. "All I know is that while I was rocking back and forth on that buoy, I kept wishing you were still an artist, still able to support yourself. Not only were you happier, it was good insurance."

She looked away from him. "You know why I stopped."

"Yes, I know why. But now, I want you to change it. If you can—" His voice became gentle. "Try, Andrea. Try for me and for Tim. And right now, while Sharon is here is a good time." He turned to me. "Mac Weiss at the charter boat place thinks there'll be work for me in a week or so, Sharon. Setting up trips for the tourists." He grinned. "Safe job, except when some

124

tourist complains about not catching any fish. So, anyway, I won't be around during the day. Andrea and I think you're very good with Tim. I can't believe the things you've done. Before he fell asleep, he kept bringing your projects for me to admire. And I saw the fort in the backyard through the bathroom window. Where'd you get those wonderful boxes?"

"They're freezer boxes. From Kreger's downtown."

"Great. Can't wait to go play in it myself."

I looked at Andrea. So she hadn't been as negative as I'd thought. I wondered what she was thinking as she continued to stare into her teacup.

"I know you're right, Larry," she said finally. "That day before they found you, I thought I was already a widow, and I thought about what that might mean. First of all, I knew I'd miss you. I can't even talk about that. And then thousands of problems went through my mind: the insurance, whether there was enough. The roof, that place it leaks when it rains a certain way. That tire on the car that's smooth. I kept thinking, no, they'll find him. Then every time I looked out the window I saw the ocean, saw how enormous it is. It's a miracle that you're here."

Larry took her hand in his and smoothed the back of it, and I knew they were thinking about Bill.

She blinked and smiled a crooked smile at him. "I'd rather paint than waitress. Or beg in the street."

All at once she looked frightened, and her eyes focused inward to something in her mind. "If I can."

"You saw her pictures, Sharon. They're wonderful. People bought practically everything she painted."

"But I thought," I started, then stopped. They were both looking at me, waiting for me to finish. "I thought you were the reason—" Now, they'd think I was nosy, too interested in their problems.

He smiled grimly. "I didn't do it. She stopped herself. Because . . ."

"Larry, don't." Andrea stood up and walked to the window, glancing at Tim as he snorted in his sleep on the couch. "I know it's been crazy," she said. "God knows how often I've tried to talk myself out of this. How much I've missed it. I've been cleaning this house as a way to fill the hours I used to paint." She waved her hand around the room and tried to smile. "Shows, too."

Her face crumpled, and her arms dropped to her sides. She came back to Larry.

He stood and held out his arms. She burrowed against him as if she were no older than Tim.

"I know it can't happen again," she whispered. "But I'm so afraid."

16

WHAT WAS IT THAT ANDREA WAS AFRAID OF? WHAT could be so dreadful that no one could talk about it? I wrote a long letter to Kate, hoping she'd come up with some explanation. But did it really matter? The important thing was that I had my job.

"You're hired for the rest of the summer," Andrea told me. "I've kept you dangling long enough. You're a good baby sitter, as well as a nice person." She smiled at me. Already, she seemed softer somehow.

"Starting to draw will be hard," she continued. "But those hours I spent at the hospital last week shook me out of old habits. I'm not going to scrub anything until we stick to it."

She bought a sketchbook and drawing pencils and, during the next few days, disappeared for hours at a time. When she got home again, she seemed satisfied. Apparently, it was going well.

"How long's it been since you drew?" I asked once.

"Fifteen months," she answered. Her voice held a sharpness that kept me from asking anything more.

Larry rescued some of her paintings from the garage and hung them in the living room, where they glowed as if glad to be out again. The whole house took on an artistic sheen, because Andrea found time to bring in flowers and sea grasses for arrangements. A Persian spread appeared on the back of the couch and lent purples and reds to the room. The windows filmed over with salt spray and there were crumbs under the table, but somehow those things didn't seem important any more.

The school board called Larry and asked him to be on a curriculum review team. It met once a week, and he wrote letters and went to the library, doing research. His job started at Deep Sea Fishing. He came home tired each evening, but we saw him grow stronger each day.

Tim's favorite thing was to fly kites with Jeremy. Next favorite was to walk with me to the pet shop downtown to tease the parrot, or to stand with our noses pressed against the aquarium. He insisted that one neon tetra recognized him and burped hello. "Sometimes, he doesn't see me right away," he told me. "Fishies need little bitty glasses, I think."

Things would have been great if Tim hadn't gotten worse with Andrea. "He's telling us something," she said one evening as I helped her with the dishes. "I'm going to start putting him to bed, story and all, from now on." She saw my face and added, "It has nothing to do with you, Sharon. It's just that I need to spend more time with him."

"I understand," I said. "I can help clean up from supper while you do that, if you'd like."

"We'll do it together, Sharon," Larry said. "I'm getting my energy back. Time to do some helping out." He snapped the dishtowel at Andrea's behind, and she flicked dishwater at him. "Want a date tonight, Baby?"

"Yes," she said. "But not the hoi polloi. I've got pencil smudges clear up my arms."

The way Larry grinned at her, I knew this must be the Andrea he'd fallen in love with.

A few days later, a letter came from Penny. Of course, I heard from Kate all the time, and from Mom, and even once from Dad. But Penny? A miracle! She'd used my letter paper from my supply at home; it was just as well she didn't write often.

"Read it to me," Tim demanded. He was going into a stage of making his nap time later and later, which was driving me and Jeremy crazy. These days, I never knew for sure what time I'd be free.

"This will be your story then," I said. I gave him the envelope to hold and began:

Dear Sharon,

See? Told ya I'd write. We have rehearsals almost every night now. I love them. The director (Bret, remember?) is turning us into pros. Remember the guy who plays Oliver? I get to do a love scene with him. We practice sometimes AFTER rehearsal too, and Mom is splitting her gourd because he's 20.

"Stop," Tim said, laying the envelope over Penny's letter so I couldn't read any more. "What's that mean?"

"Splitting her gourd? It's what mothers do when they get worried." I watched his face. "Okay?"

He slowly nodded. "Why is she worried?"

"Because she doesn't know what will happen."

"Read," he said, drawing back the envelope.

My big problem is, should I tell him how old I am? I'm afraid he won't like me any more if I do. I wish you were here to tell me what to do.

"Does she want to see me, too?" Tim asked.

"Let me read," I said. He sighed and nodded.

The costumes are groovy—drapey long sleeves and gold trim. Meadyevil. Not sure how to spell that. But it means ancient.

Can you get a day off and come see the play?

"She wants to play," Tim said. "She wants to see me, too."

The beginning of August. (I read.) *Please come! I really miss you. I keep losing things (except for weight), and how come you are the only person who knows how to find everything? Mom is freezing pie cherries, and I'm supposed to help her pit. See ya. Your sister, Penny.*

"Sposed to help her pit," Tim said. He pulled Penny's letter away from me. "That wasn't a very good story. Not long enough. Tell me a story about Penny."

I sighed and studied his eyes to see if he was the least bit sleepy. "She's pretty," I said in a low, monotonous voice. "With long curly hair that bounces when she walks. And she has dark eyes that always look happy. Her favorite color is blue-green, and when we were both little, we used to make a carnival in the backyard for all the kids in the neighborhood." All at once, I stopped because I couldn't believe I was missing Penny. Missing her fun, her excitement.

I *would* go see the play. As soon as Tim settled down, I found Andrea in the kitchen and asked her for some time off.

"Of course, you should go," she said. "You need to get away from us occasionally. Your sister sounds interesting."

131

"She is," I said. "I'm the dull one."

She turned. "Do you honestly think you're dull?"

"Sure." I shrugged.

"I think you're very creative. Some of the things you do with Tim are amazing."

I smiled at her. "Really?"

She nodded. "Really. Now put your amazing mind to work and tell where I put my sketchbook. I'm getting absent-minded."

"I'll help you look."

Tim had been in the storeroom after lunch. On a hunch, I went there and pretended I was a little boy who needed more attention. Five minutes later, I'd found the sketchbook stuffed behind boxes of Christmas decorations.

"Why?" Andrea asked. "Why doesn't he like me to draw? I wonder what he remembers?"

"Remembers?"

She shook her head, not answering, but as I went through the backyard to meet Jeremy, I saw her sitting by the window. She didn't respond to my wave. She was lost in thought, and the old frozen look was back in her face.

AS DAYS PASSED, ANDREA WORKED OUT A SCHEDULE that allowed her more time with Tim and gave me more of the housework. He seemed more content finally, and we decided we'd done the right thing.

One afternoon in late July, Jeremy, Tim, and I sat together on the living room floor, building a bridge with LEGOs when Larry walked in from work.

"Glad you're all here," he said when he saw us. "I want that fantastic concert you two keep promising me. Yesterday, I was in the backyard while you played out on the cliff. For a few minutes, I could hear real well, then the wind changed and blew the sound away. I didn't have time to sneak up closer or I would have."

"I'll run over and get my harmonica," Jeremy said. "Want to run with me, Tim?"

"We might sound better with the wind blowing part of us away," I said as I tuned my guitar a few minutes later.

Larry grinned. "We could turn on a fan."

"We'll eat in an hour," Andrea said from the kitchen. "Except for Sharon. She and Jeremy are going on a picnic. And if Tim asks to go, say no."

Larry laughed. "You don't want to take Tim?"

"Not this time. I hope that's okay."

"You have to have a little social life," Andrea said.

"But just a little," Larry said with a wink.

"Wanta play somepin," Tim said when he and Jeremy returned.

"Here," Andrea said. "This makes a nice sound." She handed him a strainer and a spoon. "Be gentle, or you'll scrape all the plate off the spoon."

"Ready?" Larry asked, sitting on the couch.

"Ready," I answered.

Jeremy's harmonica wailed out the intro we'd thought up, then my guitar came in with the three-four strum. "Don't be thinking of me all away and alone."

Jeremy's tenor and Larry's bass joined in. "On the rolling old sea, on the foreign ground."

"For I hung your sails, and I sent you to sea," I sang.

"On the dark old waters, all alone."

Andrea came to listen at the door, holding her hand under a drippy wooden spoon.

"You sound like drunken sailors," she said as we finished, then went back into the kitchen.

"Let's do it again," Larry said. "The harmony needs work."

So we did, and this time Andrea said there was hope for us.

"Do some more," Tim said, banging his spoon and sieve together.

We played a few more. It was fun to have Larry's harmony with ours. We weren't that good, but we were good enough to have fun. Finally, I looked at my watch and decided it was time to get started on our picnic. It seemed that Jeremy and I could never spend enough time together, especially lately, with Tim's irregular nap times. A whole evening together sounded heavenly.

"Be sure that hat doesn't fall into the fire," Larry said to Jeremy as we left.

I nodded. "It'd poison our hot dogs."

"A low blow!" Jeremy batted me with the bag of potato chips, and I pushed a cold can of pop against his back.

We'd made it to the backyard when Larry called us back. "Telephone, Sharon. It's your sister Penny."

"Wanta talk to Penny," Tim said and clung to my leg as I took the phone.

"Opening night is Friday," she burbled. "I want you to come. Can you get away?"

"Already? This Friday? I'd like to. I'll ask."

Andrea glanced at the calendar that hung on the back of the kitchen door. "Friday's fine," she said. "But I need you Saturday night. There's a reception at the Sandpiper Art Gallery. I really want to go . . ."

"I'll come back," I said shaking my head at Tim who was tugging at my leg.

"And plan to take a whole weekend another time." Andrea nodded her thanks to me and went back to slicing carrots.

"I'll be there," I said into the phone.

"Me too, please." Tim gazed beseechingly up at me and patted my thigh.

"Oh, Penny. Tim wants to come." I laughed. "No, Tim, you aren't ready for Shakespeare."

He began to sob, and I stuck a finger in one ear so I could hear Penny. "Wait till you see the famous love scene," she shouted.

"Is this play X-rated?" I pressed the receiver against my ear. "Tim, hush."

Andrea put down her knife and led him away. He began to wail.

"Oliver is X-rated. He whispers things to me right while we're on stage," Penny said when I could hear again. "Things that even Shakespeare didn't write." She giggled. "I'm glad you're coming. I'll get

136

your seat with Mom and Dad. Best seats in the place. And there'll be a wild party afterward. Without Mom and Dad."

"Great!" I hung up, excited about a night off from work.

"Sorry about this kid," Andrea hollered, coming back into the kitchen with Tim who was still howling. "Hope you could hear okay."

"Wish I could go," Jeremy said.

"You sound like Tim."

"I mean it. I have to make a trip to OSU to pick up some forms for housing. I could get the car maybe, and we'd drive over together."

"Jeremy! How fun! Let's do it!"

"I have to ask. I'll call Mom." In a few minutes he'd arranged it, and I called Penny back.

"You didn't ever mention a Jeremy person," she teased. "Will I like him?"

I hesitated. "Of course."

"Boy, is Touchstone going to be jealous."

"Penny, cut it out," I said. "He's just a friend."

Jeremy raised his eyebrows at me, and I blushed. Just then, Tim figured out that Jeremy was going to get to go.

"Not fair," he roared. "I want to go see Penny." He threw himself to the floor kicking and thrashing in the beginnings of a tantrum.

I quickly said good-bye to Penny.

"Scoot," Andrea said. "I'll handle this. Go on your picnic."

We scooted.

"Glad to get outa there," Jeremy said as we started down the path. "What a monster."

"He's not usually like that."

"If he was, you'd be crazy to spend another day here."

"He's sweet most of the time. We had the best time this afternoon after his nap. I gave him a big paintbrush and a pail of water, and he painted the outside of the house. Turned it all shiny. He thought it was neat. At least until it dried and got dull again."

"Plain water? What a good idea. You know what's great? Andrea. She's a different person."

"Do you suppose we'll ever find out why she stopped painting? Something awful must have happened."

Jeremy shook his head. "Maybe she painted someone's portrait and they sued her."

"Pretty funny. But that wouldn't make her stop," I said. "Not painting for her must be like not talking —or not singing. As if part of you is dead." I shivered. "Let's talk about something else."

We stepped out onto the sandy beach. "To the ocean?" he asked. I nodded, and we walked past Tim's fort and around the curve of the end of the bay.

"We've got a couple of hours," I said, noticing

where the sun was. "Maybe there'll be a good sunset tonight."

"I brought a new kite to try," he said. "A stunt kite, with dual controls."

He put the kite together while I built a fire. Amazingly enough, I'd remembered everything, even the matches and the forks for roasting the hot dogs.

"Great picnic," Jeremy said after he'd downed four hot dogs and most of the bag of chips. "What time should we leave on Friday?"

"Could we go around noon?" I asked. "I want to see Kate and go shopping. Larry paid me last week, so I can buy something glamorous to wear to opening night."

"No jeans?" He looked shocked.

"You wear anything you want. I'm going to be glamorous." I had to be, I thought, to offset the visual impact of Penny.

As if he knew what I was thinking, Jeremy said, "I'll get to meet the paragon. Will I be overwhelmed? Vanquished by her unmatched beauty?"

"Of course, you will. She snows everybody."

"Bet she can't snow me." He pushed the flaming logs closer together.

My throat was tight as I watched the flames grow stronger.

He turned to me. "Worried?"

I shrugged.

"Hey, I've got a cool head under this hat. No Shakespearean goddess is going to vanquish me."

I tried to smile.

He jumped up. "There might be enough wind now. Let's try the kite. Want to hold it for me?"

"I like this kite," I said as I picked it up. It was red nylon stretched over a diamond-shaped frame. Simple, sleek, streamlined.

"But can it fly," he said. "Let's find out. Let go when I holler."

Jeremy and I had test-flown a number of kites, but this was an instant favorite. It responded to every signal, no matter how slight, as we took turns zooming it across the sky. This kite would even touch down on the sand, then take off again.

"I can write my name," Jeremy said at last.

"Impossible. This kite isn't that clever."

"Watch the tail," he said and sure enough, after a few false tries, he wrote "Jeremy" in the sky.

"My turn." I took the controls, but it was hard to do. "It helps to have a 'y' in your name," I said. "The 'a-r-o-n' all look alike up there."

"Get ready to read." Jeremy took the controls away from me.

"J," I said. "Oh, sure, 'Jeremy' again. What now?"

"Watch," he said. "You think I can't do something different?"

"What's that?," I asked. "An 'e'?"

"No, it's an 'l'."

"Look, Jeremy. There's going to be a nice sunset."

"Don't look over there, watch the kite. This is important!"

"Jeremy. L-o-v-l?"

"That's an 'e'," he growled.

"E, s." I held my breath. "That's 'loves'?"

"Smart. Keep reading."

Over and over the kite twirled against the dark blue sky, its long tail tracing a message in vibrant red that was meant only for me. "You did it!" I said. "You made it do a perfect Sharon."

"Did you like it?" he asked, letting his hands drop down at his sides so that the kite floated quietly above us.

I went to stand beside him, and he handed me one of the controls as he put his arm around me. Suddenly quiet, we looked out at the ocean where the sun swelled and turned into a fuzzy orange ball. It touched the water and changed, flattening into a glowing pancake, growing thinner and thinner, lapped away by the sea. At last, the fiery line flickered and disappeared.

But that wasn't the end. An orange glow seeped north and south along the horizon and bled into the clouds overhead. Gold leaped toward us through the tips of the waves and washed across the sand at our feet. Jeremy was already looking at me when I turned. The gold was on him, and coming from inside him. It shone in his face that he thought I was special. It shone that he loved me.

18

FRIDAY NOON, I WAS PACKED AND READY TO LEAVE when Jeremy called.

"Sort of a crisis here," he said. "A tour bus from Los Angeles. Forty people, all crazy to buy kites. Could take an hour, maybe even more, because someone just said there's another bus following this one."

"I hear the cash register," I said. "This bunch sounds ready to finance your dad's retirement. Can I help?"

"Only by knocking out some walls to make more space in here. Thanks anyway. I'll come as soon as I can."

I put down the phone. "He can't leave yet," I told

Andrea. "And I wanted to go shopping in Santiam, to buy a dress for tonight." I waved my purse in the air. "Larry paid me, and I have to look wonderful . . ."

She rinsed her hands, dried them, and tossed the towel on the counter. So different from the old Andrea.

"I've got the perfect thing for looking wonderful. Want to see it?"

I hesitated. "Borrow something? What if I spill on it. Cast parties are noted for crudeness."

She laughed as we went upstairs. "I've been to a few cast parties. They're crazy, but they're fun." She reached far back in her closet and pulled out a long-sleeved peasant blouse, shimmery and purple! "From India," she said. "It's gauze, really cheap fabric, but then they add to it." She pulled out a skirt and draped it across the bed. It was very full, with gold and black embroidery. It was beautiful!

Maybe there was hope. I pictured myself standing next to Penny . . .

She rummaged in a drawer and pulled out a tie belt with little bells tinkling from long gold strings. "It wraps around and around. You have to have a tiny waist to wear it, and you do. Want to try it?"

Five minutes later, I was transformed. "Is it me?" I wondered aloud as I rotated in front of Andrea's mirror. "Are you sure you want to lend this?"

"It's perfect on you, isn't it," she said with a satisfied nod. "Don't worry about it. I've already worn

144

it a lot. See, there's even a little tear here in the skirt where I caught it on something. I never mended things in those days. You're going to outshine everyone. Even the leading lady!"

"It's my little sister I'm worried about," I said recklessly. The gorgeous creature in the mirror seemed capable of saying anything.

"Oh yes. The one who makes you feel dull. She must be a hard act to follow," Andrea said, searching through her jewelry box. "Aha! Like these?" She waved delicate purple cascades at me. "You have pierced ears. Try them."

I fastened the earrings on. "It's just that Penny bowls people over. Jeremy thinks I'm crazy, but that's because he hasn't met her yet."

"I haven't met her either," Andrea said. "But Jeremy's one level-headed young man. She may be wonderful, but he knows you are, too."

"I'm just afraid that when he sees us both, he'll see . . ." I shook my head at my reflection in the mirror, and the earrings winked back at me. They weren't magic; they were just glass . . .

Andrea came to stand behind me, her face troubled as she looked into the mirror. "You're standing differently now. As if you don't know how lovely you are. There, that's better," she said as I straightened. "Goodness, this is fun. It's like playing fairy godmother."

There was a thud from downstairs, and we both cocked our heads and simultaneously thought, Tim!

"I'll see what he's into," she said and ran down the stairs as I rotated once more in front of the mirror and piled my hair up on top of my head. In spite of myself, excitement began to return. I looked like a Woman with a Past. I looked exotic.

"Oh, no."

The anguish in Andrea's voice pulled me from the mirror.

She and Tim were in the storeroom. Her sketchbook lay in front of him on the floor. Papers lay scattered around him, crumpled and torn.

Andrea picked up one of the papers and shook it at Tim. "Why," she demanded. "Why did you do this?"

His face was stony. "Don't like these."

"So you ripped them and ruined them. These are mine, Tim. Do you want me to spoil your things?"

His voice rose in volume. "You go away all the time. I don't like it."

"But while I'm gone, you and Sharon . . ."

"I want *you* to wake me up after my nap. I want *you* to bring my catsup. I want *you* to cut my samich."

"You want. What about what I want." She bent and scooped papers together. "Oh dam. I liked that one." She spread a paper against her knee and then recrumpled it in disgust. "It's ruined, Tim. Ruined. This is so naughty."

"No," he said with a pout. "*You*'ve been naughty. *You*'re not s'posed to do this."

"It just seems different now," I said soothingly to Tim. "Pretty soon, you'll be used to Mommy going off to draw."

"Go away, Sharon," he hollered. "I'm talking to my mommy."

I left and changed into jeans. Andrea's purple dress and earrings went into my suitcase but I hardly knew I'd packed them. All her drawings, destroyed. Three weeks of work.

She and Tim threw the remains of the sketchbook into the trash. Then she put him to bed. They were both very quiet.

"He's still getting used to the whole idea," I told Andrea when she came back downstairs.

She shook her head. "Those sketches weren't that important. I have to think of what he needs. He comes first!"

"You have to come first sometimes, Andrea. Drawing is important to you."

"When you're a mother, you'll understand, Sharon."

That's all she would say. She started to clean the oven as if her life depended on it, squirting foul-smelling Oven Glow and ripping off paper towels.

Jeremy called to say the second bus had been a rumor and that he'd be over soon.

"I'm sorry it's so late," he said as I climbed into

his car later. "But it was worth it. The Californians just paid my tuition to OSU."

He couldn't believe that Tim had destroyed Andrea's sketchbook. "He's a spoiled kid."

"He's spoiling Andrea's life. I wish she could be happy. She's so much nicer now, Jeremy." I told him about her lending the dress. "She's gotten to be like a friend, instead of an employer. Just the same, I'm ready for a vacation." I leaned back and thought, in spite of my concern, how nice it was to leave all that tension behind. Larry would have his hands full when he got back from work.

When we got to my house, Mom and Dad were in the kitchen putting a feast together.

"It's been four weeks!" Mom said, giving me a long cozy hug. She pushed me away from her and then hugged me again. "How tanned and healthy you look. Just glowing!"

Dad's hug was just as warm. I introduced them to Jeremy. He and Dad were instantly into a discussion of OSU and went off together to pick up Jeremy's papers and to see Dad's office.

My room! How plush and feminine compared to Tim's. My whole house was enormous; no wonder Andrea and Larry had to keep everything extra in the storeroom.

"Where's Penny?" I asked when I got back to the kitchen.

Mom glanced at the clock. "She's supposed to be here. She wanted to take a nap before dinner." She waved her hand at the counter top. "Special occasion. I bought caviar."

"That gross-looking black stuff?"

She sighed. "I haven't raised you right. Tell me how everything is going with your job. You look just great! It must be agreeing with you."

"It's a challenge," I said. "Andrea has finally accepted me, but now Tim is causing problems." I brought her up to date.

"He needs a brother or sister," she said. "Only children sometimes expect too much."

"Was I that way before Penny?"

"Let me think. You must have had some adjustments. I don't remember. You've always been the easy child."

"Me?"

"Of course. You were contented. A pleasure to have around. Didn't you know that?"

"I thought Penny was more fun. More interesting."

Mom clicked her tongue and sighed. "More interesting I can do without."

I dipped my finger into the caviar and put one gross black thing into my mouth. "Tastes better than it looks," I said. "Did Kate call? I want to see her."

"She's coming for supper," Mom said.

"Here I am, da da!" Penny burst in and grabbed me. What a huggy family I had. "My sister!" she sang. "Home from the wars. Where's the mystery man?"

I grinned. "He's gone off with Dad."

"I'm supposed to rest now," she said. "I hope, hope, hope the play goes all right. There's one scene that is so iffy. If one person moves in the wrong direction, the rest of us fall totally apart, forget lines, everything! It's just awful!" She grabbed a cracker from the platter Mom was fixing and rolled her eyes. "Shouldn't do this. I'm gaining weight! Do you see it?" She whirled once around.

"No." But she was a little plumper than I remembered.

"You're so lucky, Sharon. You'll never be fat."

"No, just scrawny."

"You look great," she said and sounded as if she meant it. I'd have to check the mirror in my room to see if I'd really changed. Everyone seemed to think so.

"Wait till you see my wedding costume." She clicked her tongue and snapped her fingers. "Sexy and virginal. All in one."

"Penny!" Mom slapped the cracker box onto the counter top and shook her head.

"See ya later," Penny crowed and ran upstairs for her hour of rest.

Supper was do-it-yourself bagel sandwiches, add caviar or not as you pleased. I tried some again and almost liked it. Jeremy loved the caviar, loved Mom, loved Dad, loved Penny.

Kate ate next to me in the corner of the living room. She'd started dating Henry Wendom, and I couldn't believe it.

"He's changed a lot," she insisted. "And you have too."

"That's what everyone keeps saying."

"You look really different. Is it the purple? I didn't know you had anything purple."

"I didn't. I don't." I told her about Andrea bailing me out.

"Jeremy looks really nice," she said, looking across the room where he and Dad and Penny shared the couch. "Does he always wear that hat?"

I hadn't even noticed he had it on. I nodded. "It's glued on, I think." It was a bad time to look. He'd been talking with Dad, but just then, he bent close to Penny, doing something to her earring.

Penny left at six to get costumed and made up. The rest of us sat around and talked till seven-thirty.

As we presented our tickets at the door of the campus playhouse, the ticket taker called us back. "Penny wants Sharon and Jeremy to go backstage."

Backstage, once we found it, was quiet bedlam. People looking like olden-day lords and ladies danced western swing in one corner, to a rhythm only they could hear, since there was no music.

A dark-bearded muscular man in wrestler's tights curled up in the corner of a couch and bit what was left of his nails.

Jaques was there, pacing a side hall, speaking his lines to a long-stemmed rose. He waved and nodded and went back to pacing. Penny was in the make-up chair, being fussed over by a gorgeous young man in baby-blue skintight jeans.

"Let me down, Frederick," Penny shrieked. "It's my sister!"

The hair stylist clicked his tongue and then smiled at me, no doubt picturing the improvements he could make.

Penny threw her arms first around me and then around Jeremy. "I'm so nervous." She pulled us from person to person, introduced us, and then drew us into the main hall. "Everyone's so nervous. This is my court costume. Isn't it glorious?"

"It's beautiful."

She hugged us both again. "Oh, oh, Frederick wants me back. I'd better not make him mad. Bret will be in in a minute to give us our pep talk. You're both invited to the party afterward." She grabbed my hand and looked panicked. "Wish me good luck."

"Break a leg," I said, and Jeremy remembered that that meant good luck and echoed my words.

"See what I mean?" I said to Jeremy as we slid into our seats in the theater.

"I'm having fun," he said, and squeezed my arm. "Your family made me feel right at home. They're nice."

"You're nice, too," I said. We leaned our shoulders together as we looked at the program.

The play was funny and good. Penny was a minor character compared to Rosalind, who had the best lines and action as far as I could tell. But Penny was captivating and feminine, the perfect foil for Rosalind's antics.

Jaques was wonderfully melancholy, and when he spoke of "ladies, but young and fair," he walked into the audience to give *me* the long-stemmed rose. I almost died.

It was in the last act that Oliver saw Celia for the first time, and the much-heralded love story began.

Rosalind said, "They no sooner met, but they looked; no sooner looked, but they loved;—"

It was that way with everyone when they met Penny. No sooner met, but they looked. No sooner looked, but they loved.

Until Jeremy, I hadn't really minded. I took a quick glance at his face. He was looking. He was enjoying. I wished he was safely back in Brinton Harbor.

19

AS I RODE BACK TO BRINTON HARBOR ON THE BUS THE next day, I went over in my mind all that had happened the night before.

First of all, there was this thing about me taking the bus. Something Jeremy had neglected to tell me until rather late was that he'd decided to stay to take his math placement on Saturday afternoon. The test ended at five; Andrea's reception started at five, so there it was.

"Your dad thought I should take the test and that you could ride the bus back," Jeremy told me. "I should have mentioned it earlier, but I forgot all about it."

Needless to say, I was grumpy. Not only did I

have to ride back all alone, leaving Jeremy behind to partake of all the pleasures my family had to offer (there was even some caviar left), but I had to get up at ten, no small feat when you've been up till 4:00 A.M.

Then there was the cast party. I didn't know quite what to think about it.

It was at Rosalind's house. Someone said she had three little kids asleep upstairs. If that was true, they must have been wearing earplugs because we were loud.

As soon as the party started, Jeremy and I got separated, but since nobody was with anybody, that was okay. Right away, Jaques came up to me, and I thanked him for giving me the rose. He was really sweet. Said he was glad to see me again. We danced a few times and then had a nice conversation about Larry and how his brush with death might have changed his life.

Then there was Touchstone. He seemed to think I belonged to him and kept "rescuing" me from Jaques.

Every time I saw Jeremy, he was having a great time. He grinned and waved at me each time our eyes met, and I thought how glad I was that he was my friend. We met once at the refrigerator, and he said he was going to know quite a few folks at OSU in the fall, and that maybe he'd stop feeling nervous about it now.

155

The only part I'd had some trouble with was that he seemed to really like Penny. So, what else had I expected? As usual, she shone—dancing, talking, laughing. She was a favorite of the cast. The life of the party. Also, she was used to staying up later than I was. At two, I was wiped out. At three, I decided to leave.

I went to say good-bye to Rosalind, our hostess.

"You're whose sister?" she said, looking as tired as I felt. "Penny's? You're very different, aren't you. Do you act, dear?"

When I told her I didn't, she lost interest and resumed her exhausted trek about the room, telling everyone to "have a groovy time."

"I'm having a great time," Jeremy said, when I finally had a chance to break into a conversation he was having with Duke Senior, who was in real life a pet shop owner. He and I'd already talked about neon tetras needing glasses.

"Didn't we just get here?" Jeremy asked.

"About four hours ago. I'm about to die. If you don't want to go, I'll curl up on that couch."

He looked full of energy. "Would it be okay if I took you home and then came back? I'm really into this party."

"No problem," I answered as he turned back to Duke Senior.

Just then, Frederick, the hairdresser, came up to

me. Hairy chest showed under his unbuttoned silky blue shirt. I wondered if he arranged chest hair; his looked too good to be true.

"You have perfect bones," he murmured. "I'd like to do your face."

"I thought you did hair."

"Faces, too," he whispered. "Didn't you see my name in the program? Hair and Make-up by Frederick?" The hairy chest puffed out a little. "Tell me where you've been all summer." He backed me into a corner and bent closer. Whatever he'd been drinking smelled like salad dressing.

When Jeremy finally looked around for me, Frederick was running his fingertips over my cheekbones.

"He's telling me how he does make-overs," I gasped, hoping Jeremy would think this was interesting. But Frederick drew back.

He bowed, actually *bowed*, to Jeremy and walked away.

Jeremy did drive me home. And that was when he told me about the math placement test. Then, after one tiny kiss, he went back to the party. "I'll stay just a little longer," he said. "I've never been to a cast party before." I didn't mention that it might be crucial for him to have a good night's sleep before taking his exam.

It must have been a swell party. When Mom

took me to the bus at noon, Jeremy and Penny were still zonked out, Jeremy on the family room couch with all of us tiptoeing around him.

I supposed he and Penny had come home together. "No sooner met but they looked . . ."

So, I couldn't decide. Wasn't it the best party I'd ever been to? Then why did I feel so miserable?

In Brinton Harbor, Larry met me at the drugstore. "Andrea is very upset about what Tim did yesterday," he said. "She almost decided not to go out tonight, but I talked her out of that. I'm afraid she's changed her mind about you staying the rest of the summer. She's put her sketching things away. I'm sorry, Sharon."

He dropped me off at the house. "Getting absentminded," he said. "I've got to go back to get milk and lettuce. We're all out."

Andrea was in the kitchen. "Hi," she said. "Have fun?"

"Sort of," I answered. "Thanks for the dress. I loved wearing it."

"Did it do the trick?" she asked with a smile. "Is Jeremy still yours?"

"Not sure," I answered. "You notice he didn't bring me back."

She looked at me. "I can't believe she's that powerful. I wonder why you don't see how strong *you* are."

I shrugged, embarrassed. "Where's Tim?"

"Napping. He's getting later and later." She sighed. "Makes his bedtime later and later." She popped the bottom tray out of the toaster and brushed crumbs into the sink. Then she shook baking soda on the counter, dipped a sponge into it, and began to shine the outside of the toaster.

"Larry said you put your drawing things away."

"You and I have to talk about that. I've decided to wait a few years. Tim still needs me."

She continued polishing the toaster, turning it about on the counter till she'd shined each surface. Shining happiness for herself right out of her life.

"The day Larry came home from the hospital, you told him you were afraid to draw again," I said. "What happened, Andrea. If I knew, maybe I'd understand. I wish I knew why you have to do this."

She turned her face away from me.

"You see, I think Tim knows how afraid you are. And then he gets scared."

Her hands were still.

I went to stand beside her. "Please tell me. Maybe we could even work it out with Tim."

"Telling it won't change anything, Sharon. But all right. You deserve an explanation." With trembling hands she reached for the teakettle, filled it, and set it on the burner. She leaned heavily on the edge of the stove, facing the wall, speaking so softly I could barely hear.

"There was another baby, Sharon." She sent me

a quick look, then turned again to the wall. "Her name was Gina. When she was four months old, she died. Crib death, they said, and everyone believes that, except for me. When it happened, I'd just gotten back to painting again, for about an hour a day. I was at my easel in another room. It was past her time to wake up, and I didn't go to see what was the matter, I was so glad to be painting." Her knuckles turned white as her hands gripped the edge of the stove. "If I'd gone in to check—" She was silent. Then she turned angrily toward me. "That's the way I am when I paint. Do you see now? Do you see why I've been afraid? I lose myself. I never want to stop. That's what Tim's afraid of. That I might not come back. He said so."

I couldn't speak. I simply nodded. It all made so much sense. How awful—

"Drawing was my life, but so was Gina. I miss her so much."

Andrea was making the only decision she could. But wait! Was it the only decision? "It's still not right for you to stop," I said. "You know what you're doing? You're making a bargain. Trading away your life as an artist. Your life for Gina's."

"So be it. If that's what I'm doing, I have to. It makes me feel better."

"It makes Larry and Tim miserable."

"That's not true." She crossed her arms over her chest and glared at me.

"I couldn't believe how you changed, Andrea, when you started to draw. Larry loved it. He said that's how you used to be all the time. Don't you think it's better for Tim to have a mother who's happy? The way you were these last weeks?" My breath shuddered in my throat, and I stopped.

She looked at me for a long time. "Don't cry," she said gently. "I can tell you care about us. And it's tempting to believe you," she added. "I can't think straight. If I stop drawing, will it be bad for Tim? Or good for him? Have I only been thinking of myself?" She looked at the clock. "I'm going out for a walk. Out to think. There's an hour before I have to get dressed for that reception."

I blinked the tears away. How I wished there was a way to convince her. She'd turned her back to me and was pushing the toaster to one side, putting the baking soda away. In a strange way, Jeremy's theory about paralysis was right. But she'd done it to herself, and she could change it. If only she would.

CHAPTER

20

WE KNEW ANDREA HAD CHANGED HER MIND THE MO-
ment she came downstairs from dressing for the
Artists' Reception.

Turquoise gleamed at her ears and in a heavy
silver necklace. It was reflected in the deep blue of the
strawflowers on her kimono-style dress. A Japanese
fan was tucked into her wide raffia belt, and the silver
and blue cuffs of her sleeves draped almost to her hem.

Larry leaped from his chair; his book thudded to
the floor. "Wow!" he said, and then he simply stood
shaking his head and blinking at her as if he might cry.
He touched her shoulder with his fingertip. "You're
back," he whispered.

"Sharon's straightened me out," she said, smiling

at him. "Or maybe I was ready to get straightened out. And while I was getting dressed, Tim and I had a good talk."

She laughed at my look of surprise. "He said he was worried that I'd forget to come home someday. That I might forget he was my little boy. He does know how wrapped up I get. We made a bargain, didn't we, Tim?"

He looked up from sorting the three-by-five cards, his favorite game before choosing one. He nodded. "Mommy's going to get a little watch," he said.

"One with an alarm," she added. "Set to go off when I need to start for home. And lots of times, I'll be with Tim. He said he'd let me draw him! On the driftwood, playing in the dirt, sleeping. I've not done much with life drawing; I'd like to try it." She drew a long breath and touched Larry's arm. "Sharon made me see that I've been punishing all of us. For Gina's death. For what I was afraid was my fault. I've decided to stop it. It was selfish. You both deserve better than that." She smiled and twisted his arm around so she could see his watch. "We've got to go! I want to go hobnob with artists!"

She turned back at the door, her eyes reflecting the shades of blue in her dress, and shook her finger at Tim. "Tim Hanover, you be nice to Sharon tonight. She came back early just for you. I hope you're not sorry, Sharon."

"I'm not sorry," I answered. "I'm glad you're not mad at me. I was sort of rude."

"You don't know how to be rude," she said. "I needed to hear what you said. I want to give you a hug . . ." She paused, as if uncertain.

"Yes!" I said, and we met in the center of the room.

"You were the perfect choice," she said as we drew apart. "When I think how close we came to turning you down last June. Your letter sounded good, but the one the counselor sent about you made us think you'd be shallow, for some reason. Bouncy and fun, but . . . shallow." She smiled. "Shows you can't tell much from letters."

As she and Larry left, Tim chose his card and pretended to read it. "It says I'm supposed to play park garage."

"Is that what you want to do?"

He nodded and went to get his box of miniature cars.

I lay back on the couch and closed my eyes, listening to Tim's "putt-putting" and "broom-brooming" at the foot of the stairs, his favorite place for a "garage."

Exhaustion washed over me. Four o'clock bedtime last night. I opened my eyes long enough to look at my watch. Jeremy's test had just ended. In eight-and-a-half minutes (he'd probably borrowed my bike) he'd be with Penny. I sat up a little. If he was thinking about Penny when he could be thinking about me, he was being a jerk.

A real jerk. Surely, he could see the difference.

Andrea had said it. The things she and Larry liked about me were things Penny couldn't do. As a matter of fact, Jeremy had said the same thing, in different ways, that day long ago when I first told him about Penny. "She ought to be admiring you!" he'd said.

I lay back again. How pretty that red kite had looked as it traced his love message in the sky. He wouldn't stop being my friend. He wouldn't prefer Penny to me.

She'd be getting ready to leave the house soon to be made up and costumed. She'd really been good in the play. How could she stand all that tension? Backstage was more my style, having all the fun with none of the trauma. Choir solos were different. But, I'd changed my mind about swing choir. Kate was right. Folk choir sounded better to me now. Maybe we could do some sea chanties. There was one guy around school who had a nice deep voice. I could just hear the harmonica

The phone rang. I peeked at Tim before going to the kitchen to answer it.

"Sharon?" It was Penny.

"I was just thinking about you," I said. "You were so good last night. I never had a chance to tell you."

"We didn't have a chance to talk about anything," Penny said. "That's why I'm calling. I wanted to ask your advice. I need to know what to do about me and Oliver."

"What's the problem?" I asked. "Have you got time to talk now?"

"I've got ten minutes," she said, and I pictured her sliding down to sit on the floor in the hallway between our bedrooms. I leaned on the counter top and stared at Andrea's cookbooks.

"It's about telling him I'm only fourteen," she said. "I said I was seventeen at the beginning, and he believed me. But I have to keep making stuff up, and I'm afraid I'm going to blow it. It's hard to be seventeen when you're not, Sharon. Do you know what I mean? The part that's fourteen keeps sneaking out."

"I think you should date guys you don't have to lie to," I said. "If you can't relax with him, you ought to forget him."

She was silent a moment. "You're probably right, Sharon. It's just that he's such a doll."

"He is. But that still doesn't make it worth it, as far as I'm concerned." I smiled at a mental picture of me, Sharon, the Advisor. I should recommend Kate to Penny. *She* was the one who'd taken psychology.

"Maybe you're right. I'll try to decide. Anyway, when are you coming home again? Thought you were supposed to get weekends off every now and then."

"Soon," I said. "Andrea knows she owes me a weekend."

"Would you mind not bringing Jeremy?"

I stood up straight. "Why? What did he do?"

She laughed. "He didn't do anything. He's nice. But you and he are such a couple. Every time I looked at you, you were sending messages to each other. I want to do stuff with you and me. Like we used to. Talk—and stuff." She giggled. "Want to hear something funny? Mom and Dad were talking just outside my room this morning, and I couldn't believe how loud their voices were. I got to bed kinda late—"

"I know."

"Dad said, 'She's grown up.' And Mom said, 'She's a young woman, Dan.' And I thought they were talking about me because of the play or something. But it was you they were talking about."

"Me?" My voice was croaky. I wished I'd heard that conversation.

"And you know what, Sharon?"

"What?" I held out my hand to Tim who'd come in the kitchen looking for me. He pressed against me and ran a little car up and down my thigh. I smoothed his hair and nodded. "I'll come play with you," I whispered.

"They're right," Penny said. "You changed a lot this summer."

"It comes and goes," I said. "Right now, this young woman is about to crawl on the floor and play cars with Tim."

"I hope it happens to me someday," Penny said.

167

"Growing up that way. We'd better hang up. Wish me luck for tonight's show. We got a great review, by the way, and I got two lines of it."

"You did!" I gasped, all at once remembering the reporter from the *Santiam Post*. "I mean . . . you deserved it," I said. "Break a leg."

It was about an hour later that Jeremy knocked on the door. Tim and I had eaten supper and were back to playing with his cars.

"You came back?" I stood up, brushing off my jeans, wishing I'd combed my hair at least one since this morning.

"Of course," he said. "I live in Brinton Harbor, remember?"

"You didn't go to the play?"

"Why would I do that? I've already seen it."

"Didn't you think Penny was really good?"

"Sure, but not good enough to make me want to watch Shakespeare all over again. What'd you think, that I'd thrown you over for Penny?"

I grinned at him. "Crossed my mind. Made me worried you had poor taste in women."

"Come here," Jeremy said. He folded his arms around me and kissed me hard on the mouth, forcing me to be quiet. Tim snickered as Jeremy kissed me again, softly.

"There's something about an older woman," Jeremy whispered. "Wrinkles, gray hair . . ."

168

I pushed off his preposterous hat, and Tim grabbed it off the floor and put it on. "Now I'm the king," he said. "You have to stop that kissing stuff and play cars with me."

Jeremy and I stepped apart. Obediently, we each picked up a car and knelt to push them across the floor.

"Broom, broom," I said, and Tim nodded his approval.